Yaard and Abroad
From a Jamaican Perspective

Yaard and Abroad

From a Jamaican Perspective

CLAUDETTE BECKFORD-BRADY

AuthorHouse™ LLC
1663 Liberty Drive
Bloomington, IN 47403
www.authorhouse.com
Phone: 1-800-839-8640

This is a work of fiction. All of the characters, names, incidents,
organizations, and dialogue in this novel are either the products
of the author's imagination or are used fictitiously.

Published by AuthorHouse 03/31/2014

ISBN: 978-1-4969-0189-7 (sc)
ISBN: 978-1-4969-0188-0 (e)

Library of Congress Control Number: 2014906111

Any people depicted in stock imagery provided by Thinkstock are models,
and such images are being used for illustrative purposes only.
Certain stock imagery © Thinkstock.

This book is printed on acid-free paper.

CONTENTS

1 INVASION

A speck appeared on the horizon, slowly growing in size until it became a shape. The shape grew until it resembled a great winged creature which seemed to glide across the water, its dazzling whiteness, coupled with the glare of sun on sea, an assault on the eyes.

The entire village was watching the approach of the strange creature with varying degrees of interest. The youngest children showed no interest in either their elders or the thing out there on the water. They contentedly carried on with their game of hide-and-seek amongst the trees and the lush green foliage that reached right down to the edge of the sandy white beach. The elders gently murmured amongst themselves as to what manner of strange creature this could be approaching their shores and what its coming could mean.

As they watched, another two specks appeared on the horizon, rapidly materializing into two more of the winged creatures. They skimmed over the water at a fair speed until by and by they appeared to furl their wings and ease to a gliding stop.

Now the villagers could examine them more closely.

They appeared to be three giant sized canoes rising to an amazing height above the water. The large white wings were now reposing leisurely at ease.

Even as the elders watched, they could see signs of movement on the great canoes, and hear strange sounds. What appeared to be a man like themselves, stood on one of the canoes and made waving signals towards the natives on the beach, and opened his mouth, from which strange words proceeded.

On closer examination, the natives realised that this man was *not* like them. His skin was of a very pale hue, and the words coming from his mouth were like no words they had ever heard before. The elders, being more cautious, watched and waited, but the young men of the village jumped into their own gaily painted canoes and made for the giant canoes, whooping and shouting in excitement at this exodus from tedium.

The Taino villagers, up to that point, were blissfully unaware of the magnitude of the changes which would be forced upon them by the arrival of these strange people in their strange canoes.

The date was May 3rd, 1494. The strange canoes were named the "*Nina*," the "*San Juan*" and the "*Cadera*." The following morning, 4th of May, 1494, Christopher Columbus, with his Spanish conquistadors, would "discover" Jamaica, and start the colonial calendar rolling.

The sun set; the night drew in, and the Taino, otherwise known as Arawak, Indians retired leaving sentries to keep watch on the giant canoes. Sounds ceased as silence settled on the land; the silence punctuated only by the night noises;

crickets chirping, toads whistling, and the sighing of the sea and the breeze in the trees.

The morning dawned like a jewel; bright and sparkling in the golden glow of the sun, which shimmered on the sea with a sheen like silver. Droplets of dew glistened on the foliage and rainbow hued parrots and parakeets chased each other in the branches of the trees. The sky was an azure blue canopy suspended overhead, complimenting the whiteness of the sand and the lush green of the vegetation.

All the Taino settlements along the north coast of the island were aware of the presence of the pale-skinned strangers. Since the first sighting of the strange canoes, messages had been going back and forth along the coast, and the progress of the vessels tracked. Now the settlements to the west of where Columbus had spent the night were in a fervour of frenzied excitement. The giant canoes were headed their way!

The young Taino named Kayo, son of the cacique, listened in silence as the heated debate swung first one way and then the other. His father, along with most of the elders, was in favour of allowing the strangers to come ashore, whilst the majority of the young men were for repelling them.

From the first sighting of the giant canoes, Kayo had been filled with a sense of foreboding; a presentiment of danger; a premonition of impending doom. He had so far not taken any part in the discussions, but listened intently to both sides of the argument. Now he stood up and indicated that he wished to speak. He commanded attention immediately, not only because he was the son and heir of the cacique, soon to become cacique himself as his father was well advanced in years, but also because he was a serious and thoughtful young man, whose wisdom had been proven in the past.

"My people," he began, "I have listened carefully to the opinions expressed regarding these strangers. I have purposely refrained from taking part until now, as I wished to gauge the various schools of thought. Having concluded that we are now at stalemate, I offer my humble opinion.

"I have a most uneasy feeling regarding these strangers to our shores. I am convinced that their arrival bodes us no good, and will spell disaster for us. I do not know why I feel this way, only that the feeling is very strong within me. I believe we should protect ourselves from unknown threats, and should these strange people attempt to land, it is my opinion that we should repel them with whatever force necessary."

A cheer of assent went up from the younger Tainos, and despite the pleadings of the elders for caution, the young men would not be dissuaded. They felt threatened, and would drive these pallid people away. So they formulated their plans, and followed the progress of the three Spanish caravels as they approached from the east.

Meanwhile, on board the *Nina* the atmosphere was one of ecstatic excitement. Christopher Columbus was the happiest he had been since leaving Hispaniola where, to his dismay, he had found the fort destroyed, and the men he had left there on his previous voyage slaughtered by the natives. But this, the discovery of this Fair Isle, was some consolation. Indeed, he wrote in the ship's journal this was ". . . a jewel of an island . . . the fairest land that eyes have ever beheld; mountainous, with the land seeming to touch the sky; all full of valleys and fields and plains . . ."

And these natives were friendly, unlike the ones on Hispaniola. Look how they had come out to greet him in their gaily painted canoes.

He had decided to name the bay where he had spent the night "Santa Gloria," which we know today as St. Ann's Bay. He was now sailing westward to see if he could find a good place to put ashore. After a short while he spied a bay which looked ideal for his purpose, and he gave the order to drop anchor and man the rowboats. Hundreds of natives lined the shores to await the pale faced strangers, while scores of others put out to sea in their canoes.

However, much to the Spaniards' surprise, unlike the natives at Santa Gloria, these natives were far from friendly. As the white men approached, a blood curdling scream rent the air and Kayo, leading hundreds of Taino Indians, hurled himself at the white men, throwing sharpened sticks, and shouting and gesticulating angrily at them. A violent fight ensued, but the primitive weapons of the Tainos were no match for the crossbows of the Spanish sailors. Columbus was determined to land, so he ordered his bowmen to fire, and let loose a big dog at the natives, scattering them and sending them scurrying in panic.

Kayo tried frantically to rally his men, but the sight of the snarling animal bounding toward them, biting as he came, was too much for them, and their resistance crumbled. A number of them had already been killed by the crossbows, and it was obvious they would not be able to vanquish or repel the strangers.

Having subdued the natives, Christopher Columbus came ashore and took possession of the island in the name of King Ferdinand and Queen Isabella of Spain. Accepting defeat in the face of the odds, Kayo, and his father made themselves known to Columbus, and brought peace offerings of fish and cassava. Columbus accepted, and in return gave them "gifts" of glass beads, trinkets, and other valueless trade goods.

A kind of uneasy peace reigned, and the Spanish sailors spent several days on the island fixing their ships, and getting fresh water and provisions, before setting sail once again. Kayo was relieved to see them leave, but his premonition of disaster did not leave with them. He was sure that his people had not seen the last of the pale-skinned strangers in their giant winged canoes. He knew that they boded no good for his people, but even he had no idea of the chain of events which had begun with their arrival.

How was he to know that his people would be ill-treated; their women violated? How was he to know that they would be decimated by small-pox, venereal, and other European diseases? How was he to know that in a matter of years the Tainos would be almost extinct in Jamaica, and would be replaced as labourers by imported African slaves? How was he to know that over four hundred years of violation of human rights and base degradation of human beings would commence with the coming of these strange, colourless people?

He could not have known, and even if he had, these peace loving people would have been powerless to prevent the course of history.

So on the morning of the 9th May, 1494, Columbus in the *Nina,* and his other two ships, the *San Juan* and the *Cadera*, sailed westward toward what we now know as Montego Bay, and left Jamaica, heading once more toward Cuba. He was to return to Jamaica some nine years later, albeit by accident whilst running from a storm, bringing more Spaniards with him to settle the island, until they in their turn would be conquered by another invading force, the English.

As Kayo watched the giant canoes sail away his heart was heavy with dread. He watched them until he could no longer make out their shapes, until they returned to being mere specks on the horizon . . . .

2 NAA GAA INGLAN'

The little girl stealthily raised her head off the pillow and listened intently. The even breathing of the other two people in the bed assured her they were still asleep. Her problem now was how to get out of the bed without waking them.

There was only one way out of the bed; she would have to negotiate Granma's sleeping form and get to the floor without waking her. Last night she had told Granma that she wanted to sleep at the front of the bed for a change, but Granma had said she was too little and that she might fall off the bed.

She wished she didn't always have to sleep in the middle; after all, she *was* nearly seven, but Granma always slept on the outside. And even if Winston, her nine year old brother, had been willing to relinquish the corner, which he constantly refused to do, it would not have helped, because the bed was square against the walls on three sides of the room.

It wasn't so much that the bed was large, which it was, being a massive mahogany affair, but rather that the room was small. The bed was set high off the floor; the children could easily sit upright underneath it. But being up against three of the four walls, it left Carol with no options; she would have to step over Granma without waking her, and find a foothold in order to get to the floor.

She slowly eased herself up the bed until her bottom was resting on the pillow. Slowly, carefully, she drew up one leg, and then the other. She manoeuvred herself until she was sitting on top of the sheet, and then she started to work her way, inch by slow inch down the bed on her bottom. It would be easier to step over Granma's feet than over her upper body.

Granma grunted and shifted position, and the little girl froze, her tiny heart pounding against her ribs. *Laad Gad! Do, nuh mek Granma wake,* she implored silently. Granma gave a long sigh and settled down, and the nervous child breathed a silent sigh of relief and resumed her journey down the bed. She reached the foot of the bed, and it only remained for her to negotiate Granma's feet in order to reach the floor.

Winston was still sleeping peacefully, lying on his back with his mouth open, and snoring gently. Taking care not to disturb him or to touch her great-grandmother, the little girl gingerly stepped over Granma's sleeping form, found a foothold at the edge of the bed, and holding on to the wall for support, she lightly jumped down.

So far, so good. She knew the room door wouldn't squeak because she had oiled the hinges yesterday with coconut oil, as Granma often did. She opened the door and slipped out into the hall, taking care to close the door quietly behind her. Through the unlocked hall door, and into the yard. She'd made it!

It was still very early. The sun had not yet risen but the sky in the east was beginning to get light as she skirted the babbeque and made her way to the kitchen, which was situated several yards from the four-roomed board house.

The kitchen itself was wattle and daub, and thatched with coconut boughs. In one corner a large sooty black jester pot with three legs stood atop several large fire-blackened stones on an elevated concrete surface which signified the cooking area. On top of a wooden dresser a variety of utensils sat, whilst a few enamel cups and a large frying pan hung from pieces of wire attached to the bamboo wattle.

Carol knew that inside the dresser she would find tough crackers and hard-dough bread wrapped up in a piece of muslin cloth, and condensed milk; the can, if already opened, would be sitting in a small enamel basin of water to deter the ants, and the top tied with a piece of the same muslin cloth. She took a handful of crackers, tore off a large piece of the bread and picked up the half-full tin of milk. She placed them carefully onto the piece of cloth which Granma used to tie up the food bundle which was sent to the bush when Pappa was working there, and tied it up as best she could. She hoped the milk wouldn't dash weh.

She came out of the kitchen, and glancing once more at the house to ensure no one was stirring, she set off, walking around the kitchen side, past the gourd tree, and down the incline towards the coffee walk. She really had no idea where she was going; all she knew was that she had to get as far from the house as possible and find a good hiding place where no-one could find her until it was too late. Let Winston go to England if he wanted to; this was her home and she was not going to leave it or her beloved Granma, to go to England and live with strangers she didn't even know—even if they were her parents!

The letter had arrived two weeks ago. Uncle Dan had brought it, and she had hated him with a vengeance ever since, because her Granma, who never cried, had cried when she read it. Carol had never seen her great-grandmother cry before; did not even know that big people could cry, and had cried herself, in sympathy. Later on Granma had called her and Winston and told them that they were to go to England to join their parents. Winston had been very excited at the prospect of flying in an aeroplane, and being nearly nine, could probably remember his mother, if somewhat vaguely, but the little girl, Carol, could remember no-one except Granma who had loved her for as long as she could remember and who soothed her when she hurt.

Granma didn't want her to go to England, that's why she had cried when she read the letter and Carol determined in that instant that she would not go. However, when she imparted this very important decision to Granma—her beloved Granma who never shouted at her—she was told very severely and in no uncertain terms that she was a child and would do as she was told. Carol, feeling hurt by what she imagined to be Granma's rejection, became even more determined not to go.

Well, that was two weeks ago, and today was passport day, so she had decided to run away. Everyone knew you had to have a passport to fly, so it stood to reason that if she did not have one, she could not go. It did not occur to her six year old brain that they would not leave for town without finding her. All she knew was that if she did not have her passport picture taken, she could not get a passport and therefore could not go to Inglan'.

She made her way through the cow pasture behind the kitchen, past the big star-apple tree, through the banana walk and down through the orange, grapefruit and lime trees, taking care not to touch the thorny spikes which threatened to tear her nightdress which she suddenly realised she was still wearing. She hadn't thought as far as clothes, or even for that matter how long she would stay away. It would have to be long enough for Winston to have his passport picture taken.

She didn't savour the prospect of staying out all night because a duppy lived in the big pimento tree up on the bluff; perhaps if she were very quiet it wouldn't know she was there. Still, it was a long way off, and as far as she knew no duppies lived this far down in the coffee walk. Nevertheless she didn't relish the thought of staying out all night. Well, she would have to get through the day first; she would worry about the night later.

She found a nice comfortable spot under a guinep tree just a short distance from the coffee walk and sat down. She tore off a chunk of bread which she covered liberally with condensed milk. It was rather sticky, and much too sweet and she didn't enjoy it as much as she had anticipated, given that it was a rare treat. She was in a terribly sticky and uncomfortable mess, and on top of that she realised that she was thirsty and there was nothing to drink. The oranges on the trees back up the slope were still young and nowhere near ready, so there was no help there.

She wiped her hands on her nightie to get rid of the stickiness but it didn't help, in fact it rather made things worse as bits of fluff from the gown attached themselves to her hands. Thoughtlessly she wiped her hands across her mouth and immediately regretted it as bits of fluff transferred themselves to her lips. Chuh! This was too much; now she would have to go down to the river. Still, that might not be a bad idea—at least she could quench her thirst. If she had been thinking clearly she would have made for the river in the first place.

As she breasted the slope which led down to the river the sun burst over the horizon and illuminated the tops of the trees, bathing them in a glorious golden glow. Carol loved this time of the day when all was still except for the insect noises and the soft sound of the wind whispering through the leaves. Bird song swelled in the sweet air and the sun's rays caressed the dew which still lingered on the leaves causing them to sparkle and glisten like precious jewels.

"Oooh!" She sighed a sigh of pure pleasure and broke into a run, her two arms spread wide as if to embrace the morning. She reached the river and washed her hands and face and then drank from the clear running water. She had never been to the river this early before, not even on washing day, and the water was much colder than usual. However, she decided that she might as well take a bath, notwithstanding the lack of soap—there was a plant nearby—quaco bush—which would lather just as well.

She divested herself of her nightdress which was sticky from the condensed milk and also damp from the dew. She rinsed it out and spread it on a bush to dry, and without a second thought, plunged into the exceedingly cold river, gasping as the shock of cold water assaulted her. She briskly rubbed herself down with the handful of quaco bush which she had gleaned for the purpose, rinsed herself off, and stepped out of the river.

She was wet and cold, and her nightdress had not had time to dry, so she found a spot where sunlight penetrated the trees and jumped up and down waving her arms in the warm morning sun till she was warm and dry.

Still naked, she wandered along the river bank till she came to a gigantic lumba leven mango tree where fallen mangoes lay liberally on the ground. She picked out the firmer and less battered ones and ate lumba leven mangoes till she felt sick. She washed her hands and mouth in the river and began to retrace her steps upstream to see if her nightdress was dry yet.

As she approached the spot where she had left the nightdress she heard an ominous sound that filled her with dread and rooted her to the spot. Then she quickly crouched down behind a bush as the sound came closer.

"Is which part di bless`ed chile deh, eeh sah?"

It was Granma! How had she caught up with her so soon?

"Carol! Caroool!" Granma called. "When a ketch dat likkle wretch, yu si . . . . !" This last part to herself, but she was close enough for Carol to hear. Then she heard her brother's voice. "Look ya Granma; si har nightie here-suh."

"Carol!" Granma called again, "ef yu nuh come here to mi right nung . . . . !" She left the balance of the threat unsaid, but that in itself was more terrifying to Carol because it left plenty of room for her vivid imagination to conjure up all sorts of repercussions.

The little girl didn't know what to do. She was determined not to have her passport picture taken and even more determined not to go to England. On the other hand if she didn't show herself immediately—and even if she did—she was sure to get some terrible punishment, or a good hiding with the belt or a guava or tambrin swish. Well, whatever happened now she was sure to get a good hiding anyway, and a good hiding was preferable to going to England. If she gave up now she would probably get the beating and still end up going to England, so she ignored her great-grandmother's calls and slipped quietly away downstream, moving inland as she went.

The thought of the punishment waiting for her when she was caught, although terrifying, did not deter her from her course of action. One thing was paramount—she had to miss the passport session; what happened after that was secondary. Still naked as the day she was born she moved steadily away from the river till she came to a big black mango tree which marked the boundary between Granma's and Rasta Sammy's land.

The tree was enormous and Granma had told Carol that it had been planted by Granma's own great-grandfather, Daniel Hezekiah Henry way back in 1838 to celebrate both the emancipation of the slaves and the birth of Granma's own grandfather. Daniel had come across the land whilst exploring, after his master, a brutal man who had had him whipped on numerous occasions for trivial things, and who, disgusted at the Emancipation decree, had turned all his former slaves off his property. The name Henry was also a legacy of that same slave master.

The land was deep in the interior of the island, and very hilly terrain which made cultivation difficult, but it had suited Daniel very well, and with no-one to place any objection he had taken possession and settled his family on the land, and soon other ex-slaves had settled around him, forming a community. The black mango tree had been planted to mark where his land ended and another's began.

Carol sat down under the mango tree and pondered her situation. She felt sure she had thrown her pursuers off her trail. She would have to stay away for quite a while, she supposed. She had nothing to eat or drink but there were plenty of windfall mangoes under the tree so her lack of victuals was not an immediate problem. She was, however, feeling totally drained and exhausted, so she sat with her back against the trunk of the tree, and in a matter of seconds was sound asleep.

She came awake suddenly as something wet and warm assaulted her face. She sprang to her feet as she tried to ward off the excited dog who was now barking joyfully at seeing a friend so unexpectedly.

"Shet up; yu stoopid daag!" she hissed, knowing that its owner wouldn't be far behind, but Blackie continued unabated. Carol was just about to make off through the bush when a gruff voice brought her up sharp.

"But wait! Likkle gyal, weh yu clothes deh?"

Too late! It was Rasta Sammy, owner of the dog Blackie, and their neighbour. Carol stood still, hanging her head down, not knowing what to say or do.

Rasta Sammy was a terrifying figure to behold. A tall big boned man with a well muscled body, he appeared to be made up almost entirely of hair. Long flowing dreadlocks, black at the roots and a reddish brown interspersed with grey on the matted strands which hung down over his shoulders and reached past his waist, and a big matted beard which also grew in strands like his hair, and which, in contrast, was totally white.

He had a deep rumbling voice which was guaranteed to strike terror into the heart of even the bravest little girl, but this was belied by his twinkling, laughing black eyes and his great love for children, and in particular for Carol, whom he had known since she was born. He held no terror for her, but because she knew that she was out of order and out of bounds, she hung her head and refused to look at him.

Sammy was speaking to her again. He threw the questions at her in his gruff voice, not giving her an opportunity to answer one before he threw another. "Weh yu granmadda deh? What yu doing here by yuself suh early eena di day? An WHICH PART YU CLOTHES DEM DEH?!"

The laughter in his voice, and the gentle kindness in his eyes belied the gruffness of his tone, and it dissolved the little girl. She burst into tears, sobbing hysterically. "Rasta Sammy, dem waan sen mi gaa Inglan to mi mamma an pappa an mi nuh waan guh far mi nuh knoah dem an mi nuh waan lef Granma far a she wan a guh deh yah an shi nuh waan mi fi guh weh far shi baal when shi read di letta an nung dem waan mi guh Town guh tek passport pitcha an mi haffi run weh far mi NAA GAA INGLAN!"

She found herself enveloped in Sammy's comforting arms as she sobbed out her almost incoherent story. Sammy, however, seemed to have gotten the gist of it for he said, "Aaright, likkle Princess; juss cool. Tell mi slow; why yu nuh waan guh si yu mamma an pappa?"

"But afta mi nuh knoah dem," the little girl sobbed. "An Miss Imo seh dem nuh have nuh tree naar flowas a Inglan, ongle factry and wan cole white somet'ing name snoah."

19

"Chuh! Miss Imo should-a know betta dan to full up di chile head wid foolishniss," the Rasta man muttered to himself, then said to Carol, "Aaright, Princess; come mek I an I guh up a yaad an I-man wi' tell yu all bout Inglan. I-man did guh deh wan time, enuh."

He took the towel he was wearing on his broad shoulders and draped it around Carol's naked form and together they made their way up the hill to his house, Blackie the dog prancing around their feet. Rasta Sammy still didn't know why she was naked but he would no doubt get the full story later. Right now what the child needed was a good breakfast and some reassurance on the question of England.

It was happening all over the island. Parents who had gone to England "for a few years" to make some money and come home rich were finding that it was going to take them many years of hard work to make even a fraction of the hoped for riches. Recognizing that they would be spending many years in England, they had begun sending for their offspring, often left in the care of grandparents and other relatives, to join them. As a result there appeared to Sammy to be a mass exodus from his beloved island, for adults were still leaving in droves, and now the children too.

It was a very perplexing problem for Ras Sammy, who considered that the country was being robbed of its children, or the children of their country—whichever way one wanted to look at it. On the other hand he could appreciate the economics that pushed people into leaving to seek greener pastures, for times were indeed hard in these 1960s, as they had been for the majority of ex-slaves and their descendants since emancipation.

As they approached the house, the yard dogs set up an excited clamouring that drew a woman to the kitchen doorway. Aunt Queenie was Ras Sammy's "baby mother". Not legally married, they were, to all intents and purposes, man and wife. They had been together for some twenty years and reared eleven sons and one daughter. Their youngest, Levi, was Carol's age and she had on occasion shared Aunt Queenie's breast with him when they were babies.

Aunt Queenie was the most beautiful person Carol had ever seen. She was very tall and had an almost jet black complexion which was as smooth as silk, and she moved with the grace of a gazelle. Her long dreadlocks were always either tied up in a colourful head cloth or hanging neatly behind her head in a "donkey tail."

It was always a source of wonder to Carol how a beautiful woman like Aunt Queenie could live with a man as rough and ready as Rasta Sammy. It seemed to her that Aunt Queenie should at least be a queen and live with a king somewhere. In fact when she was younger she had thought Aunt Queenie to be the queen of Africa because Ras Sammy always referred to her as "mi African queen."

"Waapen, Carol?" Aunt Queenie addressed the little girl whilst looking questioningly at Ras Sammy.

"Har parents dem sen fi har from Inglan an shi nuh waan guh, suh shi run weh. But wha happen to har cloase dem, mi coulden tell yu. LEVI!" This to his youngest son who was lurking around the kitchen side trying to hear why Carol had no clothes on. "Levi, run guh tell Sista Fanny seh Carol deh yah. And tell har fi bring one frock fi di chile."

Levi ran off to do as he was bid and Ras Sammy addressed Aunt Queenie. "Gi di likkle princess some tea." Carol was taken into the kitchen and given some roast breadfruit and saltfish and a cup of chocolate tea. She suddenly realised that she was famished, and set about eating with gusto. While she was eating she told Aunt Queenie and Ras Sammy how she had heard Granma searching for her and had to run away leaving her nightdress.

Her friends shook with laughter when she told them how the condensed milk had caused bits of fluff to stick to her hands and mouth. But then the little girl's mouth started to tremble and she said plaintively with tears in her voice, "But mi nuh waan gaa Inglan. Mi waan stay here wid Granma an oonu, far a oonu an Granma one love mi."

Sammy and Queenie gazed in helpless sympathy at the child. It would be heart-rending for her to be wrenched away from her great-grandmother who had raised her practically from babyhood. Her father had gone to England when she was barely six months old and she had no memory of him. Her mother had gone to join him when Carol was three years old and the only vague memory the child retained was of a shadowy figure with no features, smelling faintly of sweet powder.

Every time Carol smelled that sweet powder she recalled the figure to mind, but with no degree of fondness. After all, she had gone off to England leaving behind Carol and her brother. And to make matters worse, they now had two little English sisters whom she was sure she wouldn't like. The little girl sobbed aloud, tears cascading down her cheeks. Queenie held her on her lap and rocked her back and forth, trying to comfort her. She looked helplessly at Rasta Sammy; the child's distress was real and evident. Sammy spoke to the little girl. "Look, Princess, is not love yu parents dem nevah love yu mek dem leave yu guh Inglan."

He went on to explain to her how hard times were forcing a lot of Jamaicans to go abroad when they didn't really want to, and why it was they had to leave their children behind until they could send for them later. "An is not true seh nuh tree nor flowers not there; is untruth Miss Imo a tell."

He continued, "When I was a yute-man, I did guh Inglan one time, juss afta di war. Yu know Princess, Inglan kinda aaright when di wedda nuh too cole and nuh snoah nuh fall. A nuh every day it fall neither, and when it juss done fall it white an pretty yu si, and likkle children love play eena it; all big people to."

Sammy went on to tell her about the Queen's palace, Hyde Park Corner where he had never seen so many cars in his life, and London Zoo with its monkeys and lions and elephants, until Carol almost couldn't wait to get to England!

But then Sammy became serious, for there was something important he had to say to the little girl, but how to explain so she would understand? After all, she was only six years old. Nevertheless Sammy felt bound to try. He took her from Aunt Queenie and sat her on his knee. He smiled lovingly down at her and said, "Hear I now Princess, and hear I good."

He leaned forward and scooped up a handful of dirt and held it out to her. "Yu si dis dirt?" She nodded. He let it run through his fingers. "Dis dirt is Jamaica." He touched her face with his other hand. "Yu si dis skin, flesh and bone dat JAH-JAH give yu?" She nodded again. "Dis is Jamaica. Dis dirt and yu. Dese is what Jamaica mek out-a. One not complete widout di other, yu overstan mi?" Again she nodded, although she was not quite sure what Ras Sammy meant.

He continued, "Nevah fahget Jamaica, likkle Princess. When yu deh a foreign, rememba seh yu is Jamaica and Jamaica is yu, and rememba seh oonu need one another. Gwaan to Inglan and study book, but nuh guh deh fi live, yu hear mi? A visit yu-a visit. When yu learn everyting dat Inglan have fi teach yu, yu muss come forward home to Jamaica, seen? Suh dat yu can help to buil' up Jamaica and mek har a irie place fi live, an den nuhbaddy naa guh waan leff fi guh foreign again, yu nuh seet?"

"Yes, Ras Sammy."

His voice, which had been getting louder and louder suddenly softened. "An rememba to praise JAH every day of yu life, for is Him gi yu life. Is Him gi yu food, clothes and shelta. Is Him keep yu hearty, an is Him mek yu betta when yu sick. Him love yu, and yu muss love Him back. JAH deh everywhere, an Him wi bi wid yu eena Inglan fi guide an proteck yu. Come mek wi sing wi Psalms." They all stood up and joined hands together and began to chant the Psalm Ras Sammy had taught her.

"JAH is I light an I salvation, who shall I fear? JAH is di strength of I life, of who shall I bi afraid? When di wicked, even I enemies and I foes come upon I to eat up I flesh, dey stumble an fall . . . ."

At that moment the yard dogs set up a furious barking and they all looked up to see Granma marching toward them with resolute purpose, swinging a guava switch in her hand, which Carol knew was the "Rod of Correction" and had been brought for one purpose and one purpose only. She was about to get a good hiding. Granma was gesticulating angrily and talking to herself, or possibly to Levi who was skipping to keep up with her angry strides. Carol could see that she was in a beating mood, and she began to quake visibly, so Aunt Queenie hugged her to her side tightly, while Sammy went to talk to Granma.

As he watched her come through the gate Sammy silently observed to himself that Granma was beginning to look her age, despite her still strong step and upright body. He knew she must be over seventy because she had been born before the turn of the century, and her grandfather had been a slave who was twenty years old when Emancipation came. She was still fit and strong, however, and still ruled her yard with an iron hand of discipline.

Sammy reflected that it would be equally hard on the old lady, if not more so, to lose the children. Her husband had died last year and with the children gone she would be all alone. The children were young and would adapt to their new life, but the old lady's life would suddenly be empty. Of course he and Queenie would keep an eye on her and help her along, and her own children and grandchildren, though not living on her premises, still worked her land and tended her animals, but she would still miss the children terribly.

Granma was very angry. She came storming through the gate like a ship in full sail. "Howdy, Rasta Sammy. Bring di chile come mek a tan him hide fi him!" She referred to Carol in the masculine, a peculiarity amongst some of the country people.

Sammy didn't think a beating was appropriate in view of the child's genuine distress, and now that she was beginning to see England in a different light he didn't think she would repeat the running away episode. He wondered ruefully if he hadn't painted too rosy a picture of England for the child.

He greeted Granma, taking her arm as he did so. "Greetings and Love, Mamma Francella. Come mek I an I walk an talk," and he led her away from where Carol was still trembling in anticipation of a good hiding. He spoke with Granma for some time, with Carol straining her ears to hear what was being said, but with no success. Then they returned to where Carol and Aunt Queenie were waiting.

Sammy had apparently achieved some measure of success in softening Granma's approach, for though she tried to maintain her frown of disapproval, the sight of the little girl's tear-stained, woe-begone face softened her own aged old countenance, and she held out her arms to a willing Carol, who was forthwith enfolded in that warm hug she was so familiar with.

"Aah, mi chile; I doan't waant yu to guh neither, but Jehovah God know best. Yu rightful place is wid yu mamma an pappa an yu likkle sistah dem. Come, put aan yu frock an mek wi guh up-a yaad. Too late fi guh town again tiddeh."

She thanked Rasta Sammy and Aunt Queenie and prepared to depart. Rasta Sammy hugged Carol and said, "Doan fahget weh I-man tell yu bout Jamaica, likkle princess. JAH, di Lion of Judah be wid yu fah iver an iver. RASTAFARI!"

*

That evening as she prepared for bed Carol asked Granma why she couldn't come to England with them. "Mi waan yu come wid wi Granma, far is yu one a guh deh yah when wi gaan."

But Granma explained that she was too old to leave her home and that when she died she wanted to be buried right here on her own land, underneath the star-apple tree where her parents, grandparents and her husband were all buried.

"But," she told Carol, "wherever yu are, mi chile, A will always bi wid yu, even after mi dead and gone from dis world, an A will always watch over yu suh dat nuhbaddy kyaan do yu nuh harm. And Faada God will bi wid yu all di days of yu life, if yu only believe in Him and trust Him."

As Carol drifted off to sleep that night she dreamily reflected on how lucky she was. Not only would she have Great-granma watching over her, she would also have Jehovah God and JAH, the Lion of Judah. Sammy had explained that God and JAH was one and the same person, but she couldn't quite grasp that, because Granma's God was a white man with long golden hair and blue eyes who was hanging on a wall in the hall, while Sammy's JAH was a black man named Haile Selassie who lived in Ethiopia. Very perplexing!

Well, she had no choice but to go to England, and in view of the monkeys and lions at the zoo, and Queen's palaces, it might not be so bad after all. But she wasn't going to stay long. No sah! She would do as Ras Sammy said, and learn all she could, and then come home to make Jamaica a nicer place than England, and then no more mothers and fathers would have to go to "Foreign" and leave their little children behind.

They could get her out of Jamaica, but they would never, ever, get Jamaica out of her. No sah!

3 WHERE IS JAMAICA?

Millicent Daley stepped down gingerly from the platform of the number 159 bus onto the snow-covered pavement of the sidewalk, placing her feet with extreme care; she did not want any more broken bones—a slip last winter had cost a broken leg, sick leave from work, and the resultant increase in her heating bill since she had had to be home all day for several weeks.

She crossed Brixton Road and started walking up Acre Lane, her small stout figure—made stouter by the bulky fur-lined coat she was wearing—hunched over against the swirling flakes of the still falling snow and the piercing icy fingers of the north wind. She reached the corner of Strathleven Road and breathed a sigh of relief as her house came into sight. She used her teeth to remove the glove on her right hand, and dug into her coat pocket for the house keys, quickly unlocking the front door and stepping into the welcoming warmth of her hallway, bumping the door shut behind her with her bottom.

She threw her bag into a chair and removed her other glove, then her hat, scarf and coat. Then she sat down to remove her boots and socks, pushing her feet into her warm fluffy mules with a deep sigh that was pregnant with relief and satisfaction.

She had left work for the final time. Tomorrow morning she would not have to get up early and brave the freezing cold and the icy pavements. She would not have to stand at the bus stop forever as bus after bus passed by too full to take on any more passengers. She would no longer have to put up with the ninety-minute commute, which she invariably made standing at least for a good part of the journey until the bus started discharging its passengers as it approached Central London, by which time she was almost at work and no longer really needing a seat.

But best of all . . . in just a few more weeks she would no longer have to be worrying about the cold, slippery snow, or broken bones. She would be home in Jamaica where the sun shone all year round.

Millicent worked as a legal secretary in the West End of London. She had been with the same firm of solicitors for nearly thirty years and had just completed the last day of her working life. Although she was not yet at retirement age, she had been offered a lucrative early retirement package which would enable her to leave the UK immediately and return to her own country after forty years in England.

Millicent was fifty-five years old. She had been divorced for over ten years but still remained single. Her three children were all grown up and leading their own lives in other parts of London and so she lived by herself in her three bed-roomed house. At one point she had rented out two of the rooms, but found it inconvenient to share her kitchen and bathroom, so, although the income had been helpful, she had given the tenants notice and reclaimed her home. Now the house was in the process of being sold; Millicent was building her dream house in Jamaica and couldn't wait to go home. Jamaica; her beautiful island home.

She went into the kitchen and set some coffee to percolate—Jamaican coffee, of course. Then she peeled a couple slices of yam, a small sweet potato and three fingers of green banana. She crushed garlic and cut up onions, tomatoes and peppers to add to the saltfish which had been soaking all day, and which she now flaked. Having set the meal in motion she poured herself a cup of coffee and turned on the TV in the living room.

She was watching *East-enders* with half her attention and daydreaming about returning home to live in her brand new dream house with the other half, when her attention was suddenly snapped back to the TV. *East-enders* went off-air abruptly, and was replaced by the sonorous voice of the BBC's regular news anchorman.

"We interrupt this program to bring you a special news broadcast . . .

The international wires are buzzing at this hour with the astonishingly unbelievable story of the inexplicable disappearance of an entire island in the Caribbean. Jamaica . . ."

Millicent sat bolt upright in her chair and used the remote control to increase the volume. She could not have heard right—the newscaster could not have said what she thought she had heard . . .

". . . Jamaica, the largest island in the English speaking Caribbean has disappeared from the face of the earth! As we speak, United States aircraft and ships are reconnoitring the area of empty seas between Cuba and South America, where the island nation used to be.

All attempts at communication with the island are met with silence. Emails are returned as undeliverable; telephone calls are unable to be connected . . ."

Millicent's heart seemed about to burst through her chest. This could not be. It had to be some kind of April Fool's joke in the middle of December. But this was the *British Broadcasting Corporation*—they had no time for practical jokes. She grabbed for the telephone and dialled the international code and her mother's number in Jamaica. A few clicks, and then an automated voice; *"Sorry, the number you are attempting to call does not appear to exist . . ."*

She replaced the receiver and sat staring into space. This was impossible. She switched the TV to another channel. Same news. She turned on the radio . . . same news . . .

". . . Speculation is running rife. There are no indications of any seismic or volcanic activity either in the Caribbean or anywhere else which would offer a possible explanation . . ."

"But this is ridiculous," Millicent thought to herself. "No country can juss disappear juss suh . . ." But there it was; on all the news networks and on the Teletext. It must be true. She began frantically calling family members and friends within the UK and the US. Everyone had heard the news. Everyone was in a panic. No-one could get any response from anyone on the island. It really was true!

But how could an entire island just up and vanish without a trace? Three million-plus people, gone, just like that? Her mother. Her siblings. Aunts, uncles, cousins. Friends . . . all gone—just like that. Never to be seen again. Never to be hugged again.

Her brand new, almost completed dream house. Gone. Never to be lived in! What would she do now, with nowhere to retire to? And how would she recoup the monies she had expended on the purchase of her land and the construction of her house? She would have to find another job, and worse, she would have to stay in Britain until she could arrange some alternative, like Florida, perhaps. But where would she live in the meantime, with the sale of her house almost complete?

It just wasn't possible. It had to be some ghastly mistake or some sick joke. Cuba was still there, and so was Hispaniola with its two nations of Haiti and the Dominican Republic. Why Jamaica? Where on God's earth could it have disappeared to . . . ?

Devine retribution? Punishment for all the crime and violence? The corrupt officials and politicians? The murdering gunmen, thieves and rapists? But these things were not unique or indiginous to Jamaica? If indeed it was punishment from on high, well what about the bad old US of A, or almost anywhere on earth, for that matter?

There really had to be a logical explanation. Could the island have sunk under the sea? If so, what could cause that to happen? The news report stated that there were no indications of earthquake or volcanic eruptions. What then? A giant meteorite? Extremely unlikely—such an event would have been tracked by the world's scientists and media.

It was said by scientists that some islands would disappear as sea levels rose due to global warming and the melting of the world's glaciers and icecaps. But Millicent thought this was only a threat to certain low-lying Pacific islands—not Jamaica in the Caribbean Sea.

If Jamaica had indeed been submerged it had sunk very deep, for not even the tip of the Blue Mountains' seven thousand feet peak could be detected by the United States Navy with all its sophisticated sonar and other instruments, Millicent heard a reporter say.

She thought of all the things the world would lose as a result of this strange phenomenon. Jamaica, the jewel of the Caribbean Sea; the home of Reggae music and Bob Marley. White overproof rum and Tia Maria. Jamaican coffee, Jamaican bananas and Jamaican ginger. Pimento. Jerk spices and sauces. She could go on and on. No other country on earth could replicate Jamaican music, tastes and flavours. Other places could be scenic and beautiful. Possess waterfalls and white, soft sand beaches, sunshine and blue seas. Exotic birds. Flora and fauna. But no other country in the world could ever be as unique and wonderful as the little island of Jamaica which used to sit in the Caribbean Sea.

And then there were the Jamaican people themselves. Unique and different. Brash and sassy. Who else on earth would even *think of,* let alone do it . . . ? Who ever heard of a tropical country where nine-tenths of the population have never even seen snow, entering a bobsled race? Millicent gave a bitter-sweet reminiscing smile. *But is bright them bright!*

But only Jamaicans!

And look how many words and phrases coined by Jamaicans have now become mainstream and standardised. Even listed in prominent dictionaries of the world. More than that, so many of the Queen's English words have been Jamaicanized that they had to write a Dictionary of Jamaican English!

We nuh easy!

But what was going to happen now? Millicent wanted to know what would happen to all the Jamaicans, including herself, who had worked for twenty, thirty, forty years in "Foreign" and were now ready, or would soon be, to return to their homeland. Florida couldn't take them all, and probably would rebel if large influxes of Jamaicans began to descend on them. Some might end up in the "Small Islands" of the Eastern Caribbean. But a more acceptable and permanent solution would have to be found.

"Them going to have to create a new Jamaica for us somewhere," Millicent thought. "Like they did with Israel. Mightbe somewhere in Africa."

The Rastas would love that!

Yes, Jamaica might very well be replicated on the Motherland continent. Yes; that would be fitting . . . As it was in the beginning . . .

Millicent could live with that. Some Jamaicans wanted to deny or hide their African ancestry, but not she. They could build a little Jamaica in Africa. She was sure that everything that grew in Jamaica could be grown in Africa. She was rather partial to a nice fresh piece of Negro yam or well-dry yellow yam with flaky saltfish seasoned with nuff onions and peppers and tomatoes, such as she was having for her dinner this evening. Hmm; she inhaled the spicy aroma of well-seasoned saltfish simmering on the stove.

But wait . . . That smell was not quite right . . . Millicent jumped up from the sofa and rushed into the kitchen. There was the acrid smell of burnt food; the saltfish was burnt to a crisp—black and stuck to the bottom of the small Dutch pot. All the water had dried out of the pot with the hard food, and the yam, bananas and sweet potato was burnt beyond redemption. Good thing she had caught it before the pots themselves caught fire.

This whole bizarre business of Jamaica disappearing had totally banished the memory that she had pots on the fire. Now she would have to prepare something else or go out for fish and chips, she thought grumpily as she opened the kitchen window to let out the burnt stench and let in a blast of cold air.

But outside was freezing cold and the nearest fish and chip shop a good little walk away. She could walk down to *Cynthia's Takeaway* on Acre Lane and buy some fry dumpling and saltfish, or even a fried snapper or parrotfish. Better still, she could phone one of the guys from the mini-cab office and ask them to buy and deliver—cash on delivery. She knew most of the cab drivers and had done this often in the past.

When Lloydie arrived with her order, she invited him in for a drink of warming Jamaican white overproof rum, despite the fact that he was driving. "One won't hurt, and it will warm yu up. Mek di most of it; it look like seh there soon won't be nuh more Jamaican rum, Lloydie."

"Wha mek?" Lloydie asked curiously.

"Yu nevah hear the news? Jamaica disappear. Di whole island gone without a trace. Not even the American navy with them submarine can find it. Mi t'ink everybody would be talking about a big ting like that . . . Oonu nuh hear 'bout it?"

Lloydie looked at Millicent curiously. "Weh yu-a chat 'bout, Millie?"

"Oonu nuh listen to news? Jamaica gone. Disappear into thin air. We don't have nuh island to go back to."

Lloydie burst out laughing. "Millie, is Decemba. Yu kyaan't run Tom Fool joke eena Decemba!"

"Is no joke, Lloydie. A hear it on all-a the newscast them this evening. Dem even interrupt *East-enders* to bruck the news. Is a serious thing. Mek mi find it pon the Teletext show yu."

She picked up the remote control and started searching the Teletext news listings, but couldn't find the story anywhere. She would have to wait for *News at Ten*. Meanwhile Lloydie was still talking to her. "Well I listen the news and I don't hear nutt'n like dat." Lloydie wrinkled his nose. "Is burn yu burn up yu dinner why yu send out fi dumpling and fry fish?" Millicent grinned sheepishly and nodded. "How yu manage to burn up yu food? Is sleep yu drop asleep?" Lloydie asked.

"I guess I must have dozed off for a bit, yes."

"There yu are, then," Lloydie said with a great big grin on his face. "Is dream yu dream the whole ting!"

And he went out, chuckling merrily to himself.

4 BUN

I lay with my eyes wide open staring into the inky darkness, the night noises on the periphery of my consciousness. I strain my ears to listen for the sound of the car to signify his arrival home, but encounter only silence.

Where *is* he? In these times one had to worry about so many things—has he had an accident? Been abducted by gunmen? Or . . . could it be that he has . . . *another woman* . . . ? I don't completely rule out the first two, but I fear—feel deep within myself—that it is neither one . . .

My ears prick up at the sound of a car coming up the street and I hold my breath, only to slowly exhale as the vehicle gives no sign of slowing down or stopping, but continues on past the gate. It wasn't him; the sound of the car recedes into the distance, bringing a return to the silence. I glance at the time on my cell phone screen for the umpteenth time in umpteen minutes. One forty-seven a.m. Nearly two o'clock in the morning. I return to my musings. I had to face facts—he was cheating on me. Because being out this late was not an isolated case; this was entering its third week. Every single evening, with no explanation. Just not coming home from work at his usual time—even if he

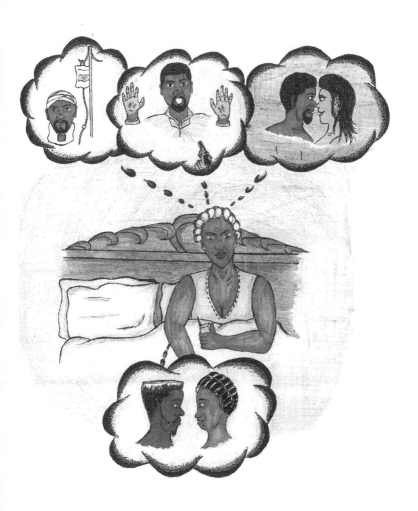

stops to have a drink or shoot a game of pool he's always home by eleven. Till lately. It *had* to be a woman.

Why is he doing this to me? Doesn't he know that I worry when he is out there at night? Doesn't he know that he is hurting me, humiliating me? Does he even care? I had asked him outright but of course he denied it. Just hanging with the guys, he said. *Till two, three in the morning, when you are a working man?* Like I was born yesterday!

And I suppose *everyone* knows except me. Knows who she is, where she lives. And the neighbours, they must all know that he is out till before-day every night; they must hear when the car pulls up and turn into the driveway, and I dread to think what they are thinking. The same as what I am thinking. Do they look at me with pity and talk behind my back? *"Poor ting; har husban' a gi' har bun."*

Oh the humiliation! Oh the mortification! Or perhaps it passes without remark since everybody's doing it. Well, everybody that is, except me.

The dark cloud of despair which has been hovering over my head for the past couple of weeks settle and make itself comfortable—it plans to stay awhile. There was no use in my trying to deny it. He was giving me "bun".

I begin to speculate about who it could be. Someone I know? Someone close to me? One of my friends, even? Somebody who laugh-up and talk-up with me every day? Is she local or out-a area? What is she like? Pretty? Younger? Slimmer? Is he just feeling jaded and bored after twenty-five years with the same woman? Going through some sort-a mid-life crisis and seeking to revalidate himself? Or is he just being a man, after all, doing what they all do and seeing nothing wrong with it? Is this the end of my marriage, or is he just having a fling?

He's had one or two before, I suspect. But nothing threatening like this one. The others were isolated and very temporary from what I could make out by careful observation. I did not challenge him about them, and they ran their course. But this is different; consistent. Every night for the past two and a half weeks. *This one is a threat.*

I check the time again. Two-ten a.m. I listen intently and think I hear the sound of an approaching vehicle—but no—it's only wishful thinking.

Two thirty-three. I must have dozed for I come awake with a start. I lie in the dark listening, trying to identify what brought me out of my doze. The neighbourhood dogs are shattering the previously silent night with howls and growls and baying. I strain my ears to hear over their serenading. I get up and go to look out of the window to the street. The moon is bright tonight. The street is deserted and the house across from us is in total darkness, and why wouldn't it be, at two thirty in the morning?

Should I call his cell phone? And say what? *"Where are you?"* The most asked question in every language since the advent of cell phones. He would *not* like that. He would know I was checking up on him. No, he wouldn't like that at all. Not at all. I lie there feeling hurt, angry and impotent. I torment myself with images of him and her, whoever she is. I visualise them making love.

"Why are you tormenting yourself like this?" I ask myself as a tear finds its way from my eye and rolls down my cheek, followed by another, and another. The dogs fall silent. Another car approaches. I hold my breath, but again

it gives no sign of stopping, and fresh tears fall as it passes and the night once again fades into silence. I speculate on the occupants of the vehicles which have passed. *Are they philandering husbands on their way home?*

My tears now turn to anger. I've given him twenty-five years of my life and three children. Worked hard at my job and made significant financial contribution to our home and lifestyle. Is he spending *our* money on her? Does he pay her rent; buy her clothes and jewellery? A car? Pay for her fancy nails and hair styles?

Anger turns to thoughts of revenge. Two can play at that game. *What's good for the goose . . .* an all a-that. A gwine give him back "bun".

I can get a man. Easily. Afta mi face nuh fava board. Nuh tree naa grow eena mi face! Gwine tek half the money from the joint account and transfer to my personal account. Should-a really tek more than half, but never mind. Gwine find somewhere and move out leave him. Tek half-a di furniture. Good thing I'm not one of those poor women who have to depend financially pon man. That's why every woman must learn the value of education and self-reliance . . .

A car is coming up the street. It's slowing down. It's turning into the driveway. It's him; he's home. The car door slams. He's unlocking the grille. I snuggle down under the sheet and pretend to be asleep. I have nothing to say to him; nothing at all; actions speak louder than words.

He will see. A gwine give back "bun"!

5 THE WHITE MAN

He was sitting six empty bar stools away. We were in the pub at Peckham Rye. I eyed him surreptitiously as I sipped my lemonade shandy and chatted with my best friend, Monique. We were lamenting the dearth of suitable black men available to us. We conceded that there *must be* a few good black men, but acknowledged that they were all already spoken for—married or living in common-law bliss with their girlfriends or baby-mothers. The ones who were left were either big time criminals or small time hustlers, drug pushers and pimps. Or else they were womanisers. Or else they were intellectually inferior.

I found my eyes continuously straying down the bar toward the man who was sitting six empty stools away. He raised his pint glass of draught Guinness and took a long drink, as if he had a colossal thirst. I watched the workings of his throat as the liquid slid down it. When he replaced the glass on the bar counter it was half empty and he had a white foam moustache on his upper lip.

There was no doubt about it; he was a very good looking man—for a white man. Tall; big boned, he exuded maleness and sensuality. Chiselled face with square jaw; dark eyes set

well apart; clean shaven cheeks; lips full and luscious . . . kissable . . . I watched in tormented fascination as his tongue flicked across the top of his lip and licked the foam moustache away.

I must have been staring. He glanced in my direction and our eyes made a quick four before mine slid away in embarrassment, but not before I had caught the smile he threw my way. An invitational smile, if ever I saw one. Oh, he was a man all right, a real manly looking man. I could go for him—except for one thing . . .

. . . He was white.

Monique was saying something to me. "What?" I asked distractedly. "That white guy down the bar," she pointed with her lips—"him look like him like yu, Bev. See him-a smile with yu."

I kissed my teeth and ate a few potato crisps, washing them down with a mouthful of shandy. I pretended indifference. "Well him could-a like likkle more. Yu nuh si-seh him white."

"Suh what dat seh?" Monique asked.

She *knew* what it said. It just wasn't done, and *well* she knew it. Even in these enlightened days of the early Eighties, and even though black men have been blatantly parading their white women for decades, culturally conscious black women just *did not* go with white men.

Oh; one could . . . if one was prepared to accept the vilification of black men (the hypocrites). Or if one didn't mind being stared at with open disdain by other black women. Or if one could ignore the hateful looks thrown by single white females (swfs) who despise you for taking 'their' men, just as you despise them for taking 'your' black men—although for the most part the white women who are with our black men are fat and ugly, or thin and scrawny. Can't really figure out why our men would go for the type when they have so many beautiful black women with "body" to choose from—but they do.

Yes, one could—if one was prepared to take the shit with the sugar.

But I wasn't.

Or *was* I?

Sometimes desperate times called for desperate measures.

Monique was still talking. "Well girl, at some point we going to have to make some hard decisions. No decent men left among our own ethnic group, so what's the alternative? Have an affair with a married man? Stay single and lonely? Stay on the shelf and end up as dried up old maids? Or explore viable options, of which I see one coming your way *right now*; you lucky devil."

She was right. I was still secretly watching him, and I saw him drain his glass and slide it across to the barmaid for a refill. Then he looked over in our direction again, and got to his feet. He passed five of the empty bar stools and came and sat on the sixth, next to me. He had a bright smile on his handsome face. Close up, I saw that his eyes were a startling black, like his hair. At least he wasn't blond and pale.

"Buy you two ladies a drink?" he asked, while staring quite openly and admiringly at me. I averted my gaze and gave a brief, "No thanks" at the precise moment that Monique said, "That would be lovely; thank you. I'll have a lager and lime, and a lemonade shandy for my friend."

I sent her a scathing glance and she smiled back sweetly at me. The white man signalled the barmaid who placed his refilled tankard of Guinness in front of him and took the order for our drinks.

I glanced around the pub to see who was seeing us at the bar with a white man. The pub was quite full with both black and white patrons, mainly in their own little cliques, but with some mixed groups. But no black women alone with white men.

My platonic friends, Larry and Duncan (both nice black men, but married) were playing darts. They paid us no attention. The drinks arrived and, short of being rude and walking away, I accepted the proffered shandy with a brief, "Thanks."

"Cheers," said the white man, holding up his glass. "Cheers," Monique and I responded; she heartily, and I, a trifle stiffly. He tried to draw me out in conversation, but I was mostly brief and rather taciturn. Monique tried to make amends for my rudeness by being particularly affable.

We saw him often after that. We always went into the pub at lunchtime, and on Fridays we would stop by in the evening after work. Bit by bit it became normal for him to join us. Bit by bit the patrons in the pub got used to seeing the three of us together, until by and by it no longer felt awkward. He offered to take us both to the pictures, and we accepted. Finally, one day, he asked me out by myself.

I went.

It wasn't bad. No-one gawked. Only the occasional rude or snide remark, mainly from black men (damned hypocrites). I went out with him again. And then again. Soon it felt quite normal.

And I was right. About his lips, I mean. They *were* quite kissable . . .

*

Twenty five years and three mixed race kids later, my eldest is married to a black man; her brother is dating an Indian girl of Guyanese extraction, and my youngest daughter has just taken up with a white man from *South Africa*, of all places. A *Boer*.

I raise objections. I don't really understand *why* I raise objections. *She* can't understand why I raise objections.

Oh, but of course she can't . . . Her father is a white man.

And I . . . ?

. . . I am still happily married to the white man I met in the pub at Peckham Rye.

6 RENT-A-DREADS

"Mawning, pretty ladies. My, my; but yu bote look suh nice. Is yu furse time 'ere?

"Ma name is Everal' an I ken show yu all di bess place to guh. Ef yu like, A ken bi yu personal tour guide. Yu evah si a sunset from Rick's Café?"

*

Negril Beach. Seven miles of soft white sands, bordered by the beautiful blue (and cobalt, and aquamarine) Caribbean Sea. Paradise it very self.

Margo rubbed more moisturising sun-tan lotion into her ample mottled thighs and sighed happily. "This is the life!" she thought to herself, as she checked out the dreadlocked man who was addressing her and her friend, Betty. The two English women had been saving for this holiday for a very long time. They were both in their fifties, and divorced. Their children were all grown up and had lives of their own. Neither of them had any responsibilities, and no-one to answer to. And they deserved this holiday.

Neither woman had had an easy life. Margo had raised her four children almost single-handedly. Her worthless ex-husband had been constantly un-employed, and spent what little money they had at the bookmakers and the pub. After the divorce she had been unable to collect any kind of maintenance from him for the children. She had had to work and raise her family at the same time.

Betty had divorced her husband because he could not remain faithful. It was one woman after another, and he had not even had the decency to try and keep his affairs secret. It was "like it or lump it" and she had definitely not liked it, so she had cut him loose.

Neither woman had remarried, although both had had a couple of brief romances. They had one other thing in common; they had both been married to Jamaican men. And even now, regardless of the negative behaviour of their former spouses, they *just loved* Jamaican men, especially those with dreadlocks. And they had it on good authority that Negril was "the place to be" if you wanted a plethora of Dreads to choose from.

So here they were, their first morning on the beach, after having arrived the day before. Both women relaxed in their beach chairs and did not have long to wait before the first of the promised Dreads appeared, strolling nonchalantly along the beach.

The two women and the Dread surreptitiously checked each other out as he came nearer and nearer, until he was close enough to address them, which he did, using a phoney American accent. Betty slid a glance at Margo, who winked at her before replying to the Dread. "Hi. You're right; this is our first tme in Jamaica; we just arrived yesterday. I'm Margo, and this is Betty."

The Dread grinned, his gold teeth flashing in the morning sunlight. This conquest was going to be easy. These women were obviously ripe to be plucked. They weren't exactly prime quality fruit, but when all was said and done, they would serve the required purpose, always supposing their purses were fat.

The one named Betty wasn't too bad. She had a pleasant enough face and a passable body, from what the Dread could see. A bit on the plump side, which was okay; Everald was not particularly attracted to skinny women, although in his line of work he could not always afford to be picky.

Margo, on the other hand, was *fat*. Not only fat, but decidedly un-attractive. As Everald watched her applying even more lotion to her already well-lotioned thighs, he noticed how blotched and mottled they were, and how large and droopy her breasts were in the swimsuit. From the size of her stomach, one could have been forgiven for thinking she was pregnant.

But generally speaking, it was usually the fat, unattractive women who were more eager to be picked up by such as him, and if he read this one right, she was more than ready to be picked. Her friend was better looking, but did not have that 'desperate for sexual attention' look that she had. He could produce a 'friend' for her, or he could work both women himself, if they were not averse to it. He hoped their purses were well lined with English pounds.

The two women, meantime, were having thoughts of their own. Margo couldn't believe they were scoring so quickly. They had been on the beach for less than twenty minutes. She supposed she shouldn't just accept the first offer, but a bird in hand was worth two in the bush, and she was taking no chances.

Betty, the more cautious of the two was thinking about what their friend Jayne had told them. Jayne was a sixty-eight year old retired business woman from Brixton, South London, who had purchase property on the island and had lived in Negril for some eight years. She had told them to beware of the "rent-a-dreads" on the beach, who preyed on lonely and vulnerable women. She had warned them not to be flattered or swayed by the "sweet talk" or the hard-luck stories the Dreads spouted; they wanted two main things— money and sex.

The money was more important; the sex was sometimes a price they had to pay as a means to their end, sometimes it was tolerable, and sometimes it was a distinct pleasure. But the money was their ultimate goal; their reason for doing what they did; it was their livelihood.

And of course they were always looking out for the main chance, where a woman would marry them and take them back to "Foreign" with her, or to send them "Western Union" or "Moneygram" when she returned home. Betty ran these things through her mind as she scrutinised the Dread, who had set to work on Margo, his skilled eye and honed instincts telling him she was the more pliable of the two.

He was not particularly good looking, Betty thought, and his dreadlocks, though long and hanging down past his waist, did not look as if they were well cared for. Parts were straggly, and they looked rusty in the sunlight. His beard was not long, but it was unkempt. His eyes were small and squinty, and red; probably from smoking marijuana.

Betty was not averse to a holiday romance; what the heck, why shouldn't she? She had been absolutely faithful to that bastard she had married until they had divorced. She had had a few dates over the years since the divorce, but she did not hop into bed willy-nilly, although if her fancy was tickled she was not reticent about doing so. But if what Jayne had told her was true, and she had no reason to doubt it, then by heck she was going to get her money's worth. She didn't think this Dread was worth whatever the price was; it was early days—she could wait a day or two and check out other prospects.

In any case he seemed to have focused on Margo, who was simpering coquettishly at him. Sensing Betty's attention now on him, he turned to her. "An you—Betty, right?—ef yu like, A could get a frien' to escaat yu, or A doan mine looking afta yu bote myself. Is up to yu."

Betty pasted on a plastic smile and began to banter with him in her Geordie accent, which she had never lost, despite twenty years living in South London. "And what makes you think you can handle both of us, then, Cock? We're a lot of woman for one man, baint that so, Margo?"

The Dread grinned broadly. They were going to play the game without too much persuasion. "I man is a whole-heap a man. A ken hangle bote of you wid ease." There was no mistaking the sexual overtone, especially since he was crude enough to grasp his genitals as he said this. They bantered some more, after which they swam, and then the Dread took them to a beach bar/restaurant where they lunched and drank rum punches and pina coladas—at the women's expense, of course—until they became silly. Everald rolled spliffs (marijuana cigarettes) for them, which, they being unused to, went straight to their heads, leaving them high as a kite. Then he suggested all three retire for a 'nap' to which the silly women, inebriated and flying high, were not averse.

He asked where they were staying. There were some places which were off-limits to the likes of him, but he was reassured when they said they had rented a cottage from a friend. The women packed up their beach stuff, and Everald found a taxi, again at their expense, and they left the beach.

The taxi driver, Blacka Dread, who was a friend of Everald's, himself had the gift of the gab and a flow of pretty words, and by the time they got to the cottage he had become a foursome with them. It seemed these fares could turn out to be very lucrative, in more ways than one; it was better than sitting in the sun hoping for passengers.

Later in the evening, sexually sated, the women were taken back to the beach where they stood and watched the sun go down. It wasn't *Ricks Café* but so what—they saw the sunset.

Then back to a restaurant where they once again paid for the meal and drinks. At no time did either of the Dreads offer to contribute. Everald, in fact, went to great lengths, and did an Oscar winning performance, in order to gain Margo's sympathy for his old sick father who needed constant medication which they were unable to afford. Despite Jayne's warnings, Margo gave him fifty pounds. They danced, drank, and smoked away the best part of the night, and in the early hours of the morning they stumbled back to the cottage, and bed.

Betty was the first to wake up. She noticed that the sun was high in the sky. She sat up in the bed and as she did so she realised that she was alone. She got up and went into the bathroom. There was no sign of her night's partner, Blacka

Dread; he had obviously gone. She knocked on Margo's door and at the mumbled response she pushed open the door and went in. Margo was alone in her bed. Everald too had gone.

"Wha' time zit?" Margo mumbled groggily. And then, "God, my head hurts!"

"Half-eleven," Betty answered. "Where are the fellas?"

"Uh?" Margo sat up in the bed and looked around the room. There was no sign of Everald or his clothes. "I suppose they had things to do," she said. "He has a sick father."

"Oh, come on!" Betty said. "You didna really fall for *that* line, didya, Hen? I thought you were only humouring him when you gave him that dosh." Margo looked slightly shame-faced. "Well, I expect we'll see them later on the beach."

The first indication that something was wrong came when they were getting ready to go and eat. Betty had showered and went to get something from her suitcase to wear. The corner, where the suitcase and travelling bag had been, stood empty. She looked around the room; perhaps she had moved them and put them somewhere else. She did not see them. She looked under the bed. Not there.

With a sinking feeling she looked at the chair on which she had thrown her handbag when they had stumbled in during the early hours of the morning. The bag was not there. She gave a little scream.

Margo came wobbling into the room. "What is it?" she asked.

"I think we've been robbed! My suitcase and handbag are gone!"

Margo hurried back into her own room and her scream confirmed Betty's worst fears. The two friends looked at each other in horror. This could not be happening to them. What should they do now?

"Let's call Jayne," Betty finally said. They phoned Jayne, whose cottage they were renting, and in a few minutes she was at the door. She was not outwardly sympathetic, although she felt sorry for them.

"I *warned* you," she said. "It's not as if you were two innocent fools who had no idea of the runnings of this place. You went into this with your eyes wide open. I have been living here for eight years and I see what goes on. You're lucky they didn't get violent with you. Some women are beaten up badly." She asked them about the Dreads.

She had never heard of one named Everald, but then she did not know all of their names. And the trouble with describing them was that the general description fit so many of them; unless they were particularly short or particularly tall, or had some other identifying feature, they were mostly anonymous. And again, some were here today and gone tomorrow.

She had lived here for eight years and had established herself. At first it had been difficult; it had been assumed by the beach dreads that she was a lonely white woman who was looking for comfort and companionship. It had taken her a long time to get them to understand that she was simply a retired woman who preferred to live in a tropical paradise rather than in cold, cold England. But they had eventually learned that she meant what she said, and she had earned the respect of the majority. Of course she was still pestered on the beach from time to time, but she had learned how to handle them. She even spoke to them using their own patois dialect.

At sixty-eight, Jayne could have easily passed for someone in her fifties. She was trim and shapely, and was a fun-loving woman who loved life. She too was a divorcee, but did not feel the need to validate herself by having a man in her life. She was self-sufficient and independent; she did not need a man to make her complete. Still, if the right man came along, she would not be averse to a relationship. It would be nice to have a soul-mate to rap with, and to cuddle up to on stormy nights (she loved a good storm), but she was not desperate and she would not go searching. If someone was out there for her, she would find him, or he would find her. She could wait. And if there wasn't, too bad, but she could live with it.

But the immediate problem was what to do about her friends' plight. She was a kind woman, and despite her annoyance, she felt sorry for them. She decided to take them to the Negril police station, where she knew the Inspector quite well. But first she decided to ask around for Everald and Blacka Dread, neither of whom was known to her. None of the craft vendors or beach dreads had ever heard of Everald or Blacka Dread. None of them remembered seeing who had been escorting the two women the previous day. The staff at the beach bar and restaurant where they had eaten remembered the women well enough, but could not remember which Dread they had been there with.

The women's hearts sank. Talking to the police was a mere formality; the Dreads would not be found. The police would encounter the same blank wall of silence, and obviously the Dreads would slide out of the area long enough for the women to leave the island and things to cool down. They did not even know if the names they had been given were the Dreads' real names; they rather doubted it.

But what were they to do for the remaining three weeks of their holiday? They had no clothes, no money, nothing except the clothes they had been wearing the previous day, and swimwear and a couple of towels which had been thrown down in the bathroom, and were now getting mouldy.

After scouting the beach area and all the local hang-outs Jayne finally took them to make the police report. All their money—cash, credit cards, and traveller's cheques were gone, as were their passports and return tickets. They had holiday insurance of course, but that was of no immediate help.

Jayne offered to lend them enough money to purchase some clothes and other necessities, and they spent the next three weeks avoiding contact with all the beach dreads, but searching every face for Everald and Blacka Dread. They never saw them.

Jayne was good enough to take them to Kingston to the British High Commission to arrange emergency passports to get them back home. While they were in the Capital, they visited the Bob Marley Museum on Hope Road and also Port Royal.

On their return to the West End she took them on day excursions around the island, trying to compensate for the ruination of their holiday. They visited Bob Marley's birthplace at Nine Miles in St Ann. They went to Lovers Leap in St. Elizabeth, rafting on the Rio Grande in Portland, and hiked up into the Blue Mountains, where they visited a coffee plantation. Jayne did all of this entirely at her own expense. She was a remarkable woman.

"This," she said, "is what vacationing in a beautiful place like Jamaica should be like. Forget about the rent-a-dreads and getting your ends off, and enjoy the pristine beauty of a tropical isle."

*

On the day of their return to England Jayne took them to the airport and they thanked her for turning their ruined holiday into a memorable occasion. They had enjoyed the excursions, and despite the fact that they had not found the holiday romances they had been searching for, they had had a good time.

But they would be sure to warn all their friends in England about the "Rent-a-Dreads" in Negril.

7 MISS 'AFICAN GEMSTONE'

Miss Jemima McIntyre was extremely upset. Furious, in fact. How dare that dreadlocks Rasta bwoy come call her African? She with her high colour, straight hair and European features! She, whose great-grandfather had been a Scottish laird, and her grandfather a planter class Jamaican who owned vast acreage.

It wasn't *her* fault that her white mother had chosen to marry a mulatto man, against the wishes of her family. And when he had run off with another woman, leaving her mother with two young children to raise alone, Jemima knew it was the *black* half of her father that had made him act that way.

But even though she got one quarter of black genes from her worthless father, the other three quarters were absolutely pure, unadulterated white. Huh! African indeed! The bwoy was an idiot.

Miss Jem's mother had instilled in her that, even though they had been reduced to the lowly status of having to 'keep shop' in order to survive, she must never forget that she was of aristocratic stock and must conduct herself at all times

with that in mind. She had lived by these precepts all her life and at seventy-three years of age was too old to change her way of thinking.

And now this Rasta bwoy with his knotted up, matted rope of hair on top of his head come telling her that if she only have one teaspoon of black blood in her, she is African! But after all!

Miss Jemima kissed her teeth in outrage, straightened her aristocratic back and glared at the Rasta man from behind her shop counter and her bifocals. "Young man," she boomed in her English educated voice, "it would serve you well were you to go and trim your hair and beard, bathe your body and change your clothes, instead of coming into my shop and telling me that I am African. I know my own family history better than you do, and I can assure you, I am of the Scottish aristocracy."

In fact the young man's clothes did not need changing, as Miss Jem noticed belatedly. He was neatly dressed in clean denim jeans and a spotlessly white tee-shirt with a picture of Haile Selassie emblazoned on the front. His long dreadlocks were neatly tied behind his head and his beard was hardly more than a five o'clock shadow. But Miss Jem did not notice this initially. She only saw a dreadlocked Rasta man who had been insolent enough to suggest that she was not only black, but African to boot.

The young Rastafarian man looked her in the eye and refused to back down. "Are you trying to deny your bloodlines, Miss Jem? My grandmother tells me that your father was a mulatto, half black and half white; that makes you at least one quarter black."

Miss Jem looked at the young man in part anger, part perplexity. She was slightly intimidated; this young man *looked* like a Rastafarian but spoke like an educated person, and he had a way of looking directly into her eyes which was most disconcerting. Her perception of a Rasta man as being dirty, unkempt and uneducated had temporarily caused her to see him that way before she realised that he was in fact quite clean, tidy and well-spoken.

She was used to people like him treating her with the respect that befitted her station, and not thinking they were equals with her. But this young man not only seemed to believe he was her equal, he actually gave the impression that he thought he was superior!

Pushing her feelings of intimidation aside, she glared at him and said, "Now look here . . . ! I am well aware of my 'bloodlines' as you call it, and as for your grandmother, she was my mother's servant, and too fast and fiesty by far. She has no business discussing my family history with you. Now take your purchase and your change and remove yourself from my shop!"

She slammed a bulla cake on a piece of brown paper, a bottle of cream soda and some coins onto the shop counter and turned her back. The young Rastafarian vacated the shop, calling out as he left, "One Love, Miss African Jem."

Miss Jem sat down on the stool she kept behind the counter. She was far more upset than the situation warranted. Why did that boy's grandmother have to dip her mouth in people's business? No one looking at Miss Jem or her sister Bridie could tell that they had a taint of black blood in them. The people in the district looked up to them and treated them with the respect that befitted their station. But now this old servant woman of her mother's had to go and divulge the dirty secret.

And why? Hadn't Miss Jem's mother treated her well as a servant, giving her food and cast off clothing to take home to her family? These Negroes could be so ungrateful! No matter what you did for them, or how you tried to help them, they never appreciated you.

Miss Jem closed up for the day and retired to her apartment behind the shop.

*

Miss Jem dressed carefully in a dignified grey linen suit, donned a small black hat which she secured to her head with a deadly looking hat pin, and finished off with black leather shoes and handbag. She checked herself in the looking glass and was satisfied with what she saw; a dignified, stately lady, as befitted her aristocratic pedigree.

She said goodbye to her sister Bridie who was minding the shop today, and stepped outside to the waiting taxi which was parked outside the shop. At her approach the driver started the engine and waited for her to get in. Miss Jem, however, seemed to have no intention of entering the vehicle.

She folded her arms and glared severely at the driver, who stared back at her impassively. When it became apparent that Miss Jem was not getting into the car, the driver sighed and said, "Lady, yu waan di taxi or yu doan waan di taxi? Time is money y'nuh."

Miss Jem drew herself up to her full height and pierced the driver with her glare. "Young man, do you not know that you should always open doors for ladies, even car doors?"

The young man grinned. He was new on that taxi route and this was the first time he had been hired to drive the old lady, but he had heard about her high and mighty ways from some of the other drivers. "Oh, sarry, Miss Jem; A nevah rememba," and he leaned across the front passenger seat and pushed the door open.

Miss Jem sighed in exasperation, pushed the door shut, opened the rear door and angrily got into the vehicle, shutting the door with a resounding slam.

As the car drove off, rather faster than she would have liked, she ruminated angrily to herself. *"These insolent young pups have no respect for their elders and betters. That bwoy knows he should have gotten out of the vehicle and opened the door."*

She *knew* that *he* knew that he should have gotten out and opened the door. She knew that he had purposely set out to annoy her. It was her lot—first the Rasta bwoy the other day, and now him. They had been sent to try her!

Aloud she said, "Please to drive within the speed limit, young man."

"But A not driving fast, Miss Jem."

"Nevertheless it is *too* fast. Please reduce your speed."

The car slowed to a crawl, while the driver grumbled below his breath that she "should-a hire one donkey kyaat." Miss Jem fumed silently in the back of the car until she could take it no longer. "Young man, kindly attempt to find the happy medium between this death crawl and your former break-neck speed! I have an appointment to keep and punctuality must be observed at all costs." The poor beleaguered driver sighed resignedly and increased the speed a little.

They arrived in the town and Miss Jem paid the driver and alighted from the vehicle in front of the bank. She dismissed him and told him she would make other arrangements for the return journey. Under normal circumstances she would have let him wait until her business was concluded and drive her back home. But she was damned if she would ever use him again.

As the car moved off and Miss Jem turned to enter the bank, some-one suddenly and unexpectedly grabbed her handbag from her grasp, pushing her to the ground in the process, and sped off with her bag and the last week's takings from the shop, which she had been about to bank.

Miss Jem was dazed but not hurt. A small crowd had gathered and some-one was helping her to her feet. She was escorted inside the bank where she was given a seat and a glass of water while some-one fanned her with a piece of cardboard.

She was beginning to come back to herself now. She sat up straight in the chair and said, "Thank you kindly. I shall be quite all right now."

"Take it easy Miss McIntyre, there's no rush. Take yu time." The voice belonged to the nice young brown skinned teller who was always so pleasant and polite. She gave him a weak smile and said, "Thank you, young man. If I may just sit here quietly while you process my transaction I would be most grateful."

She looked around her to locate her bag and the young bank teller said quietly, "I'm afraid the person who pushed you down stole your bag, Miss McIntyre."

"Ooh no!" Miss Jem let out a wail before catching herself. Then she regained her composure, glanced furtively around to see who had caught her in her unguarded moment, and said to the young man, "Then I shall have to change my plans. I was going to make a deposit of the proceeds from my business, but now I shall have to make a small withdrawal instead. My bank book is gone with my bag, are you able to facilitate me, nonetheless?"

"Of course, Miss McIntyre, everyone here knows you. There will be no problem. How much would you like to withdraw?"

Miss Jem was about to give the young man the figure when a commotion drew their attention. They looked toward the door to see two dirty, sweaty, bedraggled men, one of them a Rastafarian, entering the bank with a small entourage of people following behind. Some-one pushed something at Miss Jem and she realised with joy and relief that it was her bag, a little the worse for wear, but essentially intact. She rummaged quickly inside and satisfied herself that all was as it should be. Her wallet and the money in the small canvass drawstring bag were still there, although she had no opportunity to count it. Some-one was saying to her, "See'm 'ere, Miss Jem, si di dutty t'ief 'ere."

Miss Jem looked up, straight into the eyes of the Rasta man who had berated her about her bloodlines. "You!" she ejaculated. I should have known!"

She stared at him scornfully. He obviously had had to be restrained by force. He had a bloody nose and his clothes were torn and dirty as if he had been rolling around on the ground. His accomplice looked to be in even worse shape than he.

Miss Jem addressed herself to the young bank teller. "I'm not at all surprised that this Rasta is the thief. Just the other day he was extremely rude to me in my shop. He and his accomplice must have been watching me and realised that I bank the profits every week. People are usually robbed on their way *out* of the bank, not on the way *in*. He must have been watching me."

Miss Jem glared icily at the two dirty looking men and demanded to know if anyone had called the police. The nice young bank teller was saying something to her. What was that?

"Miss Mac, you don't understand. Is not the Ras who rob yu. Him run down the robber and drag him come back here, and get back yu bag fi yu. And he had to fight to get it back too."

"What's that yu seh?" Miss Jem was confused. "Is not this dirty dreadlocks boy who stole my bag? Then who?"

At this point the police arrived on the scene and handcuffed the culprit before taking him away. The sergeant took a statement from Miss Jem and before leaving, addressed himself to the heroic Rasta who had chased down the thief and caught him. "Good work, Ras. A gwine need a statement from yu and yu gwine have to come-a court fi give evidence. Come down-a station when yu ready."

"No problem, Sarge," the Ras replied. Then he turned to Miss Jem and asked, in the educated voice which had so intimidated her, "Are you alright, Miss Jem? He didn't hurt you?"

Miss Jem did not know where to look. This young man, whom she had been berating scornfully was not the thief at all; moreover, he had taken it upon himself to chase the thief, getting hurt in the process, but bringing back both thief and booty. And she had publicly castigated him. And now here he was solicitously enquiring after her well-being.

She knew what she had to do. She must apologize publicly and give the boy a reward. She stood up and looking the young Rasta man directly in the eyes, she said, "Young man, I have misjudged you and done you a grievous wrong. I owe you not only an apology, but my sincere thanks and eternal gratitude. And thank you for your concern; no, I am not hurt."

The young Rasta smiled, and his eyes lighted up his whole face. Miss Jem thought to herself that he was not a bad looking young man after all. If he would only trim and comb his hair he would be quite handsome for a dark-skinned man. She found herself smiling back at him.

"Well my young hero, if you will present yourself at my shop at your earliest convenience I will see to it that you are adequately rewarded for your efforts on my behalf."

The Rastaman replied with dignity, "Thank you Miss Jem, but the only reward I need is to know that you are unhurt. Perhaps you will allow me to see you home?"

*

SERVE!"

Miss Jem went into the shop to serve the customer. Her lined old face broke into a smile as she recognized the young man standing on the other side of the counter. "Well hello, Ras; it's good to see you. How is your grandmother?"

"Howdy, Miss African Gemstone. Granny is fine, thanks, and she sends you her best regards. How yu do?"

They exchanged further pleasantries and the young man left, after paying for his purchases. Miss Jem had never been able to persuade him to accept a reward for retrieving her bag from the would-be robber, and this had further endeared the Ras to her. They had become firm friends and from time to time they would hold discourse—sometimes fiery discourse—on various topics, and Miss Jem was constantly surprised at the young Ras's intelligence and the extent of his knowledge; he was obviously well read.

Their friendship gave Miss Jem a new lease on life; she had found someone who was worthy of her intellectual attention. And she had come to accept his habit of calling her "Miss African Gem" as a compliment of sorts; he obviously held Africans in high regard. In addition she rather liked the spin he put on the word by adding "stone"; Miss African Gemstone—it made her feel quite precious.

Their friendship had also softened somewhat her tough, austere persona. Everyone in the community noticed a softer, kinder Miss Jem, and the children occasionally found sweets mixed in with their mothers' change after their purchases. And often, now, she would allow regular and well known customers to 'truss' which she had never been known to do formerly.

A few bad-minded people with smutty minds was sure there was something more intimate than mere friendship going on, but neither Miss Jem nor the young Rasta paid any attention to it. *They* knew what their friendship was all about, and they were above idle gossip. And as Miss Jem said often to her sister, Bridie, "That young man is a credit to his family, and if at first he appeared rude and insolent, he has certainly redeemed himself. I would be proud to call him my son.

*

Miss Jem's funeral was well attended. Bridie had died the year before, and having no other kin, Miss Jem—anticipating

71

her own demise—had left with her attorneys instructions for her burial and the disposal of her estate. She had named the young Ras as sole beneficiary.

She also left him a letter in care of her attorneys, which thanked him for the pleasure he had given her during the last years of her life, and she signed it, *Miss African Gemstone.*

8 AFTER THE BIG RAIN

"It was afta di big rain. Di river did come down and flood di districk. Everybaddy was gone down to see how di river cover di bridge and wash weh Marse Linford and Miss Gertie house. And in di miggle a di excitement Mimi and Lucilda catch a big fight and bring down murder and bad-mindedness pon di districk.

And all because Mimi accidentally mash Lucilda corn toe."

Over the years whenever anyone referred to the events which occurred that October they invariably began with, "It was after the big rain . . ."

It had been an excessively rainy 'rainy season'. The rains had begun in mid September and by the middle of October people were despondent and tempers were frayed. It seemed the rain would never stop. Crops and animals had been washed away and the residents of Top Valley were stranded, as the only way out was by way of an old wooden bridge which was now under water.

Things were just as bad for those in Bamboo Valley. The river had risen higher than anyone in living memory could recall. Even Miss Imo who was ninety years old, and had lived through many hurricanes, had never seen it this bad. The one road leading out of the district was washed out and no-one could get to market, even had there been any produce to sell. The local shop had run out of just about everything, and if Deacon McCleod had not braved what was left of the treacherous road and driven his old truck into Cedar Town for rice, sugar, flour, corn-meal, salt fish and tinned mackerel, many people would likely have starved.

But one day toward the end of October the rain stopped. The clouds broke and the sun came out. One by one the residents started emerging from their houses like animals coming out of hibernation. With few exceptions, they headed for the river to see how high the water was, and to see the now empty spot where Marse Linford and Miss Gertie's house use to be.

Excitement was high. Everyone was glad to be outdoors after being cooped up inside for so long. There was a lot of good natured pushing and shoving as people strained to see the river, without getting too close to the slippery bank.

Suddenly, above the excited babble of the crowd a strident voice gave forth, "Jesas Chrise, di gyal mash mi corn toe!"

Mimi had found herself perilously close to the rivers edge and had rapidly backed up. She felt herself step on somebody's foot and was in the process of turning to apologise when her jaw met a powerful open handed slap. "Gyal, yu mash mi corn toe, yu ole elephant yu!"

Now Mimi was what was commonly referred to as a 'mampi', being some three hundred pounds in weight, but was quite comfortable with it. To be called an elephant, however, was far from comforting, not to mention being

boxed in her face, and especially as she was about to apologise. She doubled her fist and with three hundred pounds of force behind it, felled Lucilda, her assailant, to the ground.

Now, the ground was extremely soft and muddy and it took Lucilda a few seconds to find purchase and gain her feet, but when she did, without hesitation she launched her herself fearlessly upon the much larger Mimi, and there ensued a wrestling match.

The crowd's interest now rapidly shifted from the river and focused on the two fighting girls who were rolling around in the mud. Lucilda was much lighter then her adversary, which, by definition, made her the more agile, and was now sitting on Mimi's chest while pounding her with her fists. Screams, shouts, and expletives were flowing freely while the crowd split into two cheering sections.

Then Mimi managed to grab a handful of mud and splattered Lucilda's face. The advantage went from one to the other and back again, until at last some of the more responsible members of the community succeeded in separating the antagonists. But it was obvious to everyone that it was far from over.

"A gwine chop up yu whats-it-whats-it-not!" promised Lucilda.

"Anytime yu ready, gyal; anytime yu ready!" Mimi was not intimidated. Both women were escorted away, and the crowd, no longer having any interest in the river, drifted after them.

Later that evening, Mimi's baby-father, Leebert, went to Lucilda's house to try and pacify the situation. "It was a accident, Lucy. She nevah mash yu toe fi purpose."

But Lucilda would not be pacified. "Accident, mi back foot! Accident or not, shi muss look weh shi deh step. Anybody evah mash corn fi yu? Yu know how it hat? An' den bright enough Fi guh slap mud eena people face. Afta raal!"

"But according to how I hear it," said Leebert, "is yu lick har firse."

"An' it should-a done desso," stated Lucy firmly. "Shi mash mi toe, mi bax har. Fair exchange."

"Well ahright den," Leebert agreed, "mek it done now. Wi is neighbours; mek wi try live in peace nuh?"

Lucy replied, "If it done, well and good, but if shi come mell wid mi, mi a-guh fight, for mi nuh fraid a she." And with that Lucilda went into her house and shut the door.

*

A few days later, the sun having made travelling a little easier, Mimi was on her way to the town when she happened to see Lucilda bent on the same mission. "Hey, maaga gyal," she accosted Lucilda, "si mi here; come chop up mi whats-it-whats-it like yu promise."

"Yu baby-faada come beg fi yu, suh A gwine gi yu a bligh," Lucy responded, giving Mimi a sneering grin.

"Bligh, yu mumma! A fraid yu fraid!" Mimi challenged.

This was too much for Lucilda. She pushed her hand into her pocket and it emerged with an ice-pick. Mimi too, seemed prepared for war, for a knife had found its way into her hand. The girls rushed at each other, stabbing frantically. Mimi took a superficial cut to her face and another on the forearm, and the fight continued. But suddenly, Lucilda was lying on the ground bleeding profusely, with Mimi standing over her in triumph. "Dat wi teach yu," she crowed. "Nex time yu don' mell wid mi!"

By this time people had long noticed the commotion and a small crowd had converged on the two fighting girls. "My God! Mimi kill Lucy! Somebaddy get one kyar, quick. Wi have to get har to aaspital before shi bleed out!"

Somebody knelt over Lucilda to examine her. "A t'ink shi dead a'ready. Si deh, is right in har heart shi get di cut!"

"Doan' move har; nuh touch nutting. Somebody better guh fi di police. Weh Mimi deh?"

Mimi had left the scene without anyone noticing. She returned to her home where Leebert was giving the children their breakfast.

"What happen Mimi; yu kyaan' get nuh veekle fi guh town?" he asked, and then he saw the blood on her. "God almighty Mimi, nuh tell mi seh yu and Lucy ketch up again!"

"Leebert, A tink A kill Lucy."

Before Leebert could respond to this shocking statement, there was a knocking on the gate and the dogs started barking. Mimi sat like a statue, and after staring in disbelief for a second or two, Leebert went outside. Pastor Blake and Deacon McCleod, flanked by the entire community, were standing there. Suddenly it dawned on Leebert that Mimi could possibly be telling the truth.

"Leebert, where is Mimi?" Pastor Blake asked.

"Shi inside, Pastah. Is what happen, sarr?"

"Well, Leebert, Am sorry to have to tell you this, but Mimi stab Lucilda, and it look like shi dead. Clement gone fah the police and doctor. Lucilda people them threatening to kill Mimi, so I am here to keep the peace till the police get here."

As he was speaking Lucilda's two brothers, Nyah and Niney, came up brandishing cutlasses. Pastor Blake stepped in front of them and said, "The police will handle this, Niney. Them soon come."

"Pastah, if yu nuh waan get chop, move out-a di way. Wi naa deal wid nuh police," Nyah said angrily.

Pastor stood his ground. "One way or the other you will deal with the police, for if yu do har anything, is you the police gwine to take away. Now be sensible and let the law take its course."

A few moments later the police jeep drew up and two officers alighted. Pastor Blake turned his attention to them. "Good morning Sergeant; Constable."

"Morning, Pastor. Where is the perpetrator?"

"Lucy dead fi true, Sarge?" someone in the crowd asked.

The Sergeant ignored the question and waited for the Pastor to reply. "She is inside the house, Officer. Is Lucilda certified dead?"

"She dead," Sarge answered shortly. He and the Constable went through the gate to the door where Leebert was still standing, seemingly in a state of shock.

As the officers approached, Leebert roused himself and said, "Is self defence, Affissa. Lucilda did trett'n fi chop up Mimi. Shi was juss a defend harself. Si deh, shi get cut to."

"Get har a lawyer and save it fi court," the sergeant answered brusquely, and pushed past him into the house, emerging a short while later with Mimi. They put her into the jeep and drove away and the crowd gradually dispersed.

Mimi pleaded self defense, and because the ice pick was found clutched in Lucilda's hand, and because several witnesses testified that Lucilda had threatened to chop up

Mimi after the fight at the river, Mimi was acquitted of murder but convicted of manslaughter and given a suspended sentence and probation.

But for months afterwards Mimi's children came home from school with black eyes and bloody noses, earned defending their mother's reputation, and themselves, from Lucilda's children.

And to this day, though still neighbours, Lucilda's family and Mimi's family do not speak to each other, and the community still talks about what happened after the big rain.

And all because Mimi accidentally mash Lucilda's corn toe.

9   A DISASTROUS DAY

I was late already. The damn alarm hadn't gone off— or maybe it had and I just hadn't heard it, or maybe I'd forgotten to reset it—I don't remember, but anyway it failed to go off. When I surfaced, bleary-eyed, I found to my dismay that it was nearly eight-thirty.

Shit! I was conducting interviews today and my first appointment was at nine-thirty. I had one hour in which to have my bath, get dressed, comb my hair, put on my make-up and get from Thornton Heath to Brixton.

It couldn't be done. I'd have to phone and tell Andrea, my Personnel Assistant to start phoning the candidates and put their appointments back one hour. The first candidate was probably already on his way; Andrea would have to apologise on my behalf, ply him with coffee, and ask him to wait. I hoped she could reach everyone else before they set out.

I was still very tired from last night; I had intended to leave the party by at least midnight, but with the sound system blasting out Sugar Minott and Barrington Levy and Dennis Brown, and the way the deejay juss a ride the rhydm suh sweet, and then this really nice guy checked me and he bought me pink champagne and gave me a wicked draw of sensimelia—well, when I had finally left I had been shocked to realise that it was past four in the morning.

I was tipsy on pink champagne and rum punch, and charged high on marijuana and music. The guy (can't remember his name—never seen him before) had been touching me up in a dark corner and we had eventually ended up on the back seat of his car after he had driven it round to the next street which was devoid of party-goers and therefore more private . . .

Afterwards we had returned to the party where I couldn't find my friend Odette who I was supposed to be giving a lift home, and so I got into my car and drove myself home, a little the worse for drink, but without incident. I had dropped onto the bed fully clothed, only kicking off my shoes, and fallen into a drink and weed induced sleep.

So maybe the alarm *had* gone off . . . maybe I just hadn't heard it.

Anyway . . . whatever . . . I was late already.

I wasn't really hung-over, but I felt groggy and there was a slight ache above my eyes; I needed a really hot bath to open up my pores and maybe let out some of last night's toxins, as well as to try and remove the scent of my indiscretions, but I would have to make it quick. Afterwards I dressed in a grey linen suit and tackled my hair. I didn't know what to do with it. It was thick and unruly and hard to comb, a legacy from my Nigerian father and my Trinidadian (Indian) mother. I brushed it vigorously and tied it back in a ponytail. That would have to do.

I didn't have time to make up my face properly, so I just rolled on a little mascara and dabbed on a little lipstick and

rouge. I couldn't find a clean pair of tights so I retrieved what I considered to be the cleanest of the ones discarded for the wash and slipped my feet into a pair of four inch stilettos. I picked up my briefcase, handbag, and keys and opened the flat door. I made my way along the landing and down the flight of stairs to the ground floor, and then out through the street door, where I stood gaping in unbelieving stupefaction.

Betsy was gone!

Betsy was my car—I know, I know; unoriginal as hell, but suits me just fine—anyway, what I was gaping at was the empty space where *Betsy* should have been but wasn't. Where I had parked her shortly after four this morning. Where she should be now, but wasn't. I glanced up and down the street. Maybe I had parked her in the wrong place in my half tipsy state . . . Unlikely, but still . . .

No, she wasn't up the street. Or down. *Someone has stolen my Betsy.*

I stood uncertainly for several minutes, confused as to what I should do. The ache above my eyes gained in intensity. I put the briefcase down on the sidewalk and put my hand to my head. I would have to phone the police of course, and phone back Andrea and tell her to cancel all the interviews and reschedule them for some other day. I supposed I could call a cab and still make it to work, but the quicker I got the information to the police the better the chances of finding *Betsy*. I turned round and went back up the stairs to my flat.

After I had given the police all the details pertaining to the vehicle I proceeded to work. By this time it was way past ten o'clock—nearer eleven—and since all my appointments for the day had been cancelled I did not feel the need to rush, so instead of getting a mini-cab I decided to ride the bus from Croydon into Brixton.

By the time I got to Brixton it was lunchtime and I was feeling so pissed off that I decided to forget work completely and just chill for the rest of the day, so I walked up the Front Line to buy a draw of weed and then made my way to the squats off Acre Lane. I heard the rumble of the bass-line long before I reached the dilapidated old house which was being squatted by some of my Jamaican Rasta bredrin who didn't mind the fact that I was half Nigerian and half Trini. Shit; I felt more like a Jamaican more time, anyway . . .

So whenever I wanted to cool out I would seek out my bredrin and we would smoke some herbs and have serious reasonings. I rang the doorbell which sounded like a fire alarm so it could be heard above the music that was constantly blasting from the turntable. All the houses along this stretch of road were occupied only by other squatters, so there were no 'neighbours' to be disturbed or to complain to the police about loud music.

I saw the curtain at the front window twitch as someone sneaked a peak to see who was at the door, and then Rueben let me in after cracking the door an inch or two and peering out. The stench of ganja hit me with a blast and I idly wondered what he would have done had it been the police or other unwelcome visitor. Inside the house the smell was even more acute and a pall of smoke hung thick in the air like a cloud. One could get 'charged' without even smoking a spliff . . .

Rueben, along with Issachar, Naphtali and Asher were passing a chillum pipe amongst themselves, while Sister

Judah and Sister Benjamin were sharing a hand-rolled spliff. This squat was a hangout mostly for the Twelve Tribes of Israel members, but all who wanted to 'reason' were welcome, so long as you brought your own weed. 'Joker-smokers' who begged a spliff, then when you give them one, they ask for piece-a cigarette and Rizla paper too, they were not encouraged.

I greeted them. "Love, mi bredrin. Irie Sistren."

"Love, mi Sistah."

"Irie Dahta."

I sat down on a giant bean-bag cushion and took out the brown paper twist with the quarter ounce of weed I'd just bought on the Front Line. "Buil' a spliff," I offer it to Sister Judah who had just handed back the one she was sharing with Sister Benji. I commenced to build a spliff of my own.

Benji wanted to know how comes I wasn't at work on a workday. I told them about my car being stolen. Straight away the bredrin said they would put out the word and get all the members across the city to look out for it. Rueben phoned a few bredrin in Peckham and Dulwich, and some in North London. They in turn would phone other bredrin, and so people all over London would be looking out for *Betsy*.

I took a deep puff of my spliff, sang along with Bob Marley and the Wailers as they chanted down Babylon, and felt a little better.

I stayed at the squat till late into the evening—there was nothing to rush home for. Naphtali cooked up a wicked ital stew and several other bredrin and sistren passed through. By this time my quarter ounce of weed had been exhausted and I contributed £15.00 to the kitty (since I had a good job and could afford it) so that Issachar could run down to the

Front Line and buy some Sensimelia or Lamb's Bread, or even Columbian Gold, which I rather liked.

At about nine-thirty I prepared to leave. One of the bredrin offered me a lift down to Brixton station where I could get a train to South Croydon or even a bus if I wanted to, but I didn't fancy the walk home from the other end, so I opted for a mini-cab and phoned for one; I was spending recklessly today.

I was in the process of putting on my coat when a terrific pounding on the door stopped me in mid-motion. I knew it couldn't be the cab so soon and anyway I recognised the trademark knock. A cold sick feeling came over me as I heard the accompanying words. "POLICE! OPEN UP!"

Inside the front room a mad scramble was taking place. A brown bean-bag cushion was speedily unzipped and all the contraband, including the chillum pipe, which was mercifully empty and cold, shoved down into it. It wasn't a foolproof hiding place and would easily be detected if they decided to empty out the beans, but it was the best that could be done on the spur of the moment. I dipped into my coat pocket and came out with the twist of brown paper containing a couple of spliffs for my bedtime and breakfast in the morning, and dumped them into the cushion along with my packet of Rizla.

Issachar had gone to the window and was peeking through a chink in the curtains. The knock would have to be answered. Even if they missed seeing the light through the heavy velvet curtains which hung at the window, they must definitely have heard the music before it had been quickly shut off. Rueben gave one quick glance around the room and went out to answer the knock.

We all strained our ears to hear what was being said at the front door. The police could not fail but notice the stink of ganja which pervaded the entire house, not to mention the pall of smoke which perpetually hung thick and motionless in the passage. If they came in we would all be in deep shit. If they arrested me I would be in even deeper shit at work. Might even get the sack. I prayed fervently in my heart to any and every god that existed.

Rueben had gone out the front door and pulled it up behind him, talking to the officers on the doorstep and so their voices were muffled. The rest of us waited in an agony of suspense and impatience to find out what had brought the police here and whether we were in trouble.

Suddenly I heard Rueben's voice raised in indignant protest and at the same time the front door slammed open against the wall and before I knew what was happening the room was swarming with police. Rueben was shouting, "Hey Babylon, weh di raas claat oonu-a do? Oonu kyaan't come in here come a harass I an I suh . . . !"

But they were already in. Some of the bredrin tried to put up a fight but the police were not playing and they quickly overpowered and handcuffed the bredrin, giving them some kicks and licks for good measure. Some of them started to search the room; they'd obviously had experience with bean-bags before, as they did not attempt to search them, but put them into the police van which was standing by, and into which we were also herded. We were taken to Brixton Police Station, while several officers were left to make a more thorough search of the house.

We were kept waiting at the station for several hours before they confronted us with the contraband which had been retrieved from the bean-bag. All eight of us were charged with possession of marijuana and other paraphernalia related to drug use. Rueben and Naphtali were charged with assaulting a police officer and resisting arrest. I don't know if it was because I was the only bald-head but I was fingerprinted, processed and given a court date, then released on my own recognisance. Or maybe it was because I was the only properly employed one. I was loath to leave the others, but I had no choice.

By this time it was well past one in the morning and I slowly walked to the minicab office on Stockwell Road to get a cab home to Thornton Heath. When the cab dropped me off outside my house I felt a pang as I looked at the empty space where my *Betsy* was usually parked. My being arrested and charged was all the fault of the dirty rat who had stolen *Betsy*. If I could only get my hands on that stinking skunk . . . !

*

I was driving a loan car that my insurance company had lent me while they processed my claim. I had conducted my interviews at work and selected a new Chief Buyer for the Purchasing Department, and all in all things were looking good.

I had attended my court hearing and swore that I was not responsible for any of the contraband and had only arrived a minute ahead of the police. I pointed to the fact that I had my coat on when they arrested me, which should tell them something. I vehemently denied taking part in any illegal activities—I was a responsible Personnel Officer for heaven's sakes, with my career and reputation to consider.

My Rasta bredrin and sistren were kind enough to corroborate my story, and I was let off with a stern warning to watch who I kept company with in the future, but was mortified when my name appeared in the newspapers with the story, and people at work saw it. It was no consolation that they wrote that the charges against me had been dismissed. The others pleaded guilty and were fined.

*

We never did find *Betsy*. I got a new car through the insurance and I took care to avoid the squats up Acre Lane for a very long time. I didn't want a repeat of that disastrous day which had started with me oversleeping and finding my car missing, and ended with me being arrested and charged for possession of marijuana.

That had been a real disastrous day!

Oh, I must remember to set the damn alarm . . .

10 FI WI MANGO DEM

"Wi nuh drink caafi-tea, mango time;
Care how nice it may be, mango time;
At di height-a di mango crop,
When di fruit dem a ripe an' drop,
Wash yu pat, tun dem dung, mango time."

The loud, off-key strains of the Jamaican folk song shattered the golden silence of the shimmering, early-June, Sunday afternoon. Prior to the assault on the silence, the only sounds that had graced the ears of Miss May had been the chirping and chattering of the birds that socialised in the orange tree outside her living room window.

Miss May leaned her head to one side to listen better. If she didn't know differently, she would swear that the singing was coming from right inside her front yard. But of course it couldn't be. She lived alone, and today was not the gardener's day, and besides, the gardener was a taciturn old man who never smiled, and rarely spoke, never mind sing.

Miss May got up from the day-bed she had been lounging on, and went to the window to look out into her front yard. The singer, whoever he was, had heard her unspoken plea, and the singing had stopped. The orange tree was devoid of birds; the strident tones of the singer had obviously scared them away, but the absence of the birds was compensated for by the snowy-white blossom which sent a heavenly fragrance wafting through the open window and into the living room.

The garden looked serene in the golden glow of the late afternoon sun. The bougainvillea along the front wall ran a riot of colours; from pale pink through to the deepest reds and purples, and from rose through to burnt orange, all accessorised by the snowiness of the white variety.

The border on one side of the driveway boasted many-hued crotons, and red and white hibiscus, or 'shoe-black' as they are commonly known. Several patches of Impatiens and Joseph Coat grew in the shade of tall Anthurium Lilies, while baskets of orchids hung from the limbs of various trees.

Miss May smiled as her eyes and heart revelled in the beauty of her garden. Her eyes continued their journey around the yard, passing over the St. Julian and the East Indian mango trees, which were laden with ripe and turning fruit, past the patch of peppermint and fever (lemon) grass under the sweet-sop tree, and came to rest on the large overhanging branches of the Haden mango tree which extended several feet over her fence from the tree in the yard next door.

The entire tree was well laden with ripening fruit and the branches which protruded over the fence and into Miss May's yard were bowing down low under the weight of the fruit they bore. She had picked as many of the ripe fruit as she could reach, but there were many more beyond her reach. She would have to wait till her son came by to pick the rest, or get some of the youngsters who were always begging for fruit.

As Miss May looked at the tree she noticed something strange. Although there was no breeze, the tree was doing a kind of dance; the leaves were shaking, and one limb was practically touching the ground, rising and falling as if . . . Miss May went closer to the window and peered closely at the dancing tree limb.

"But you ever si mi trial!" Miss May marched briskly from the house, out onto the veranda, pushed open the grille and stepped out into her front yard. She strode purposefully across the lawn to the fence separating her yard from the next door premises and stood beneath the dancing branch, which was just above her head height. She glared up into the leaves and demanded to know, "And just what yu think yu doing, Sarr?"

The branch dipped and the leaves danced, and Miss May retreated a step, although she was not within reach of the branch. Then a bare foot appeared, followed by a leg in cut-off jeans pants, and then another foot and leg. Finally a torso in a torn merino, and then a head came into sight as the person sat on the limb of the tree, one foot dangling and the other wedged into the space between two limbs. The combined weight of the man and the fruit caused the branch to come down to Miss May's head height.

The elderly woman and the young man stared at each other; Miss May in stunned silence, the young man with an insolent grin on his face. Before Miss May could gather her wits sufficiently to speak, the man spoke.

"Maaning, Godmadda. Jus' picking dem few mango here. Nutten naa gwaan fi mi, and A figga A kyan sell two mango and mek two shilling, yu si mi?" The insolent grin remained in place.

"Well, of all the nerve!" Miss May was almost incoherent with outrage. "First of all, young man, I am *not* your Godmother, and secondly, how yu mean to be picking *my* mangoes to guh and sell? These mangoes don't belong to yu; they are in *my* yard . . . !"

"Is not your mango tree, Lady. It deh een-a fi-wi yaad; a *fi-wi* mango dem."

"Is not suh it guh." Miss May begged to dispute his statement. "The tree might be in your yard, but these branches that hang over into my yard belong to me, together with any fruit they bear. Your grandfather never give mi any problem in all the thirty years wi live beside each other; *he* knew these mangoes belong to *me*."

The young man yawned rudely without covering his mouth. "Pappa dead and gone; him did too saaf, but is we run tings now, an' right now, mango a sell, and mi need di money. Suh I gwine finish pick dese mangoes and get out-a yu way."

Miss May was weak with impotent anger, but what was she to do? She could not *physically* prevent the man from picking her mangoes; she was sixty-eight years old and of small frame. What she needed was 'backative'; someone to stand up for her, and let this out-of-order young man know that his insolence would not be tolerated and neither would the stealing of *her* mangoes. But she had no such backative to hand. She retreated indoors, defeated for the moment.

But Miss May was a woman of indomitable spirit. She would not accept defeat without a fight, but she would have to choose her battlefield and plan her tactics. She picked up the telephone and called her son, Calvin, who lived a few chains down the road. Calvin would deal with the trespasser; he was a strong, big-boned man with an intimidating appearance, and he was an attorney-at-law. Calvin would know what to do.

In a few minutes Calvin's SUV pulled up in front of the house. Miss May immediately took him over to the mango tree, which was still dancing and dipping from the activities of the facety young man. Calvin said authoritatively, "Stop pick those mangoes and come down out of the tree!"

A few tense moments elapsed, and then the first bare foot reappeared, followed by the rest of the body. This time, instead of sitting on the branch the man dropped to the ground in front of them.

"Waapen, Godfaada?" he enquired, before Calvin could speak. "A not doing anyting wrong, Sarr; juss picking mi mango dem. A fi-wi mango dem."

He spoke in a tone of reluctant respect, but hung his head down and refused to look directly at the person to whom he spoke. Miss May opened her mouth to speak, but Calvin raised a hand to silence her. He spoke to the bedraggled young man.

"These mangoes belong, under common law, to my mother by virtue of the fact that they are on *her* side of the fence. The fact that the tree is in your yard is entirely irrelevant, because in order to reach the limbs to pick these mangoes yu have to venture *over* the fence, which, in effect, means that you are trespassing on my mother's property.

"Furthermore, even if the mangoes did belong to you, there is nothing wrong with being a good neighbour and sharing the bounty. Look how much fruit yu have on your side of the fence. When yu grandfather was alive there was no dispute with him over the mangoes; it was share and share alike. We were good neighbours."

The young man was not impressed, as was evidenced by his bodily demeanour, but he was too much in awe of Calvin to be openly defiant. Nevertheless, he spoke his mind. "Look here, Sarr; if good neighbour is what yu want to be, why oonu don't share some-a oonu money wid us. Nutting naa gwaan fi mi, an' mi have pickney fi sen guh school and bill fi pay. If oonu a-guh grudge mi di two mango dem, di lease oonu kyan do is help mi out wid some cash."

Both Calvin and Miss May were taken aback by the bold effrontery of the man. Calvin recovered quickly, as befitted his profession as a lawyer. "But yu bright and facety to! Is hard work provide my family with what wi have; wi never born with gold spoon in our mouth, nor get nuh hand-out. Yu young, strong, and able bodied. Why yu don't find some gainful employment that will provide a living for yu family? Why yu don't join the army or something? The pay good, and the discipline even better."

The man sucked his teeth and without another word, swung himself back up into the tree where he retrieved a fine-bag half filled with mangoes, and retreated along the limb till he got back on his side of the fence, where he vacated the tree. Calvin and his mother stared after the retreating man in confounded consternation. Miss May finally found her voice.

"Well, from I was born . . . ! What a facety bwoy! Well, if the mangoes belong to him, then so do all the leaves that the tree shed on this side of the fence. In future when the gardener rakes up the leaves and 'drop-mangoes' I will see to it that they are returned over the fence to their rightful owner!"

Calvin reproved her. "Two wrongs don't make a right, Mamma. Yu nuh have any need to descend to fi-dem level; I *know* yu bigger than that. A gwine pick some of the mangoes fah yu, and yu 'low him the rest. If it that important to him, let him have them."

Calvin picked a couple of dozen fit and turned mangoes and found one lovely ripe one nestling amongst the leaves which the poacher had missed seeing. He proffered it to his mother, saying, "Yu can eat this one today; it ripe to perfection," but Miss May refused it. She had made up her mind that she would not eat any of the mangoes from that tree in future, but she would pick as many as she wished to give to the neighbourhood children who frequently came begging for mangoes, and the facety bwoy could go to the devil!

The next afternoon, Miss May was dozing on her day bed when she was jerked into full consciousness by a loud raucous buzzing sound which seemed to come from her front yard. She got up and went outside to investigate, and was just in time to see the Haden mango tree branch, which protruded over her fence, come down, to land with a crack and a crash, onto her peppermint and fever grass. The buzzing sound ceased as the power saw was turned off, and a loud, pregnant silence filled the air.

Miss May was too shocked to move, let alone to say anything. She gazed in astounded silence at the large piece of mango limb with many secondary branches attached, and which was still loaded with young and almost fit mangoes. The limb had come to land with the main part resting on the fence, and the end branches and leaves in Miss May's herb garden.

The silence, which in reality lasted only a few seconds, seemed to stretch into eternity, but finally it was broken by voices from next door, which galvanised Miss May into motion. A loud angry voice was shouting. "God Almighty, Clovis! Weh yu chop off di mango limb fah?"

Miss May recognised the voice as belonging to the mother of the facety mango thief. She moved toward the fence, galvanised by the voice and her burgeoning anger, but was arrested by the voice of the young man, Clovis, answering his mother.

"Juss cool, nuh Mamma; wi ha' whole-heap-a mango lef'. Nuh worry yuself." His voice held no note of regret for his wanton act of destruction. His mother's querulous voice continued, and Miss May, who had been ready with angry words of her own, waited her turn, and listened to the dialogue from across the fence.

"But weh yu chop it dung fah? It wasn't troubling yu. Is bad-mind yu bad-mind. Yu nuh good, bwoy! Yu-a fi-mi pickney, but yu nuh good! Is a sin, wha' yu do!

"Yu nuh have nuh right fi deh 'arass Miss May; is ovah t'irty 'ears she an' Pappa live side-an-side, and nevah a cross word. When A was a chile, shi was always good to mi, and now yu come here come-a trouble di woman. Mi shame a-you!"

Miss May felt slightly mollified at this vilification of the young man by his own mother, but still felt it incumbent upon herself to have her input. She covered the short remaining distance to the fence and called, "Miss Dorette?" to the young man's mother. The woman approached the fence and rushed into speech.

"Laad Gad, Miss May, A sarry fi what di bwoy do. A nevah have nuh idea seh him would-a do suppen like dat when mi hear him deh grumble bout yu an di mango-dem. A shame suh till A kyan barely look pon yu!"

Miss May had known Dorette since she was a child. She did not blame her for what had happened today, although in truth, some little blame could be applied for the way the boy had been raised without the proper amount of discipline. Nevertheless, she absolved Dorette. But the boy was a different matter. Miss May wanted justice, and truth be told, revenge. She was only human, after all. She launched into speech.

"A don't blame yu, Miss Dor, but A don't want yu to feel nuh way when A have yu bwoy up in court. Even though the mango tree is in your yard those are my mango branches him cut down."

The young man spoke before his mother could respond; "A have every right fi cut dung di limb. A fi-wi mango tree, an a fi-wi mango dem."

But later, when Miss May instructed her son Calvin to start proceedings against the young man, she was disappointed by his response. Calvin said that in point of law, any neighbour having a tree which breaches another's property, has a duty to keep that tree trimmed and clear of his neighbour's property. In the case of fruit trees, which are of benefit, by mutual agreement, the neighbour may be excused from trimming the tree. However, if that neighbour wishes to cut off the overhanging branches, for whatever reason, spite included, he could do so if he wished, because it is his tree.

Miss May was outraged. "But yu said all of the overhanging branches belong to me, Calvin. I distinctly remember hearing yu seh-suh."

"I said *the fruit* belonged to you, Mamma. Let it be. What's done is done, and although it's a sin what he did, still, it's their tree; let it be."

Miss May was loath to let it be, but she had no choice. But that boy could not be allowed to get away scot-free. "Well, him have to pay to have the limb removed, and have my garden cleaned up and my herb bed rehabilitated." Calvin replied that he would make sure that the bwoy came over and did the work himself.

Miss May did not want the boy anywhere on her property, and protested that he should be made to pay out of his pocket, where it would hurt him most, but Calvin, who was a Deacon in his church, and a good practicing Christian, told her that "to err is human; to forgive is Devine." Miss May, who was also a good Christian, decided that, *just for today*, she would rather be human than Devine. Forgiving would be most difficult; almost impossible.

The young man was not chastened by his being made to clear the limb and tidy the garden, and went about it with a cheerful whistling, which fed Miss May's anger. But there was nothing she could do, so she sat on her veranda and watched him work, making sure that he did not help himself to any fruit from her garden. Miss May was a kindly woman, and willingly gave away scores of mangoes every year, when she could quite easily get them sold, but she was damned if she was going to let this boy have even one of her mangoes. She glared balefully at him as he worked.

The following Sunday at church, Miss May prayed for forgiveness for her anger and vindictiveness against the young man, and resolved that she would forgive him for the terrible thing he had done, sinful though it had been.

Henceforth, whenever she saw the young man she would greet him cordially, and not hold a grudge. After all, she still had plenty of mangoes of her own; she could afford to forgive the poor sinful soul, poor thing. And she would pray that God would cleanse him of his sinful and insolent ways.

A few weeks later Miss May was startled to hear her name being called from next door. If she didn't know better, she would swear it was the facety young man, but this voice sounded rather pleasant. "Hello, next door. Are yu there, Miss May? Could yu spare a minute of yu time?"

Miss May went out into the front garden and went up to the fence. The space where the mango branch had been was still obscenely empty, but there was nothing to be done about that. Let bygones be bygones.

Miss May had been right; it was the facety young man, Clovis; only now, he looked quite different. He wore a clean starched white shirt tucked into black pants, and polished black shoes. His hair, which had previously been bushy and uncombed, as if he had intentions of becoming a Rasta, was now cut low and had a clean, 'just washed' look.

Miss May was surprised to see the change in the young man, and it was not only in his dress. His very demeanour was the opposite of his previous attitude. He greeted her cordially as she approached the fence. "Good afternoon, Miss May. A hope A not disturbing yu from anyting too important, but A have something A want to seh to yu."

Miss May returned the greeting with like cordiality and waited for the young man to proceed. He met her gaze squarely, and said, "Miss May, A want to tell yu how sarry I am for cutting down the mango limb. It was a wicked and spiteful ting to do, but A want yu to know dat yu kyan get anyting yu waant from ovah here-suh, anytime at all, whether mango or orange or anyting at all."

Miss May gazed at the young man in amazement. Could this be the same bad-mannered and bad-minded bwoy who had been so insolent? If so, something miraculous had happened to change his demeanour. The young man gave her the answer to her unspoken question.

"Miss May, A don't know if is your prayers, or Mamma own, but Jesas work a miracle eena mi life, and mi get Saved. A want to invite yu to mi Baptism next week. And any time yu want any Haden mangoes, just seh di word, for the bounty that God provide should be shared by all-a wi. Fi-mi mango dem now belong to yu as well, Miss May.

"No more *fi-mi* mango, but *fi-wi* mango dem."

11   JUSTINE'S REVENGE

The throb of the plane's engines suddenly swelled to a roar and then it was moving swiftly along the runway, gathering speed as it went, faster, faster, until it finally became airborne and began to climb at an angle.

Justine stared unseeingly out of the window as the lights of the airport and Kingston city receded, and the plane banked and headed out over open waters leaving the island behind, along with her hopes and dreams and a good chunk of her money. If only it were as easy to leave the memories; those bad ugly memories, but no; they would be travelling with her for some time to come, if not for the rest of her life.

The plane levelled off and the seat-belt light went out, but she remained buckled in. A flight attendant was coming down the aisle pushing a drinks trolley and she asked if she could get some rum and coke. She ignored the other passengers in the row with her—the man had briefly tried to start a conversation but she had been terse and unresponsive and he had soon turned away and struck up a conversation with the female passenger on his other side, who was more receptive and rather talkative herself.

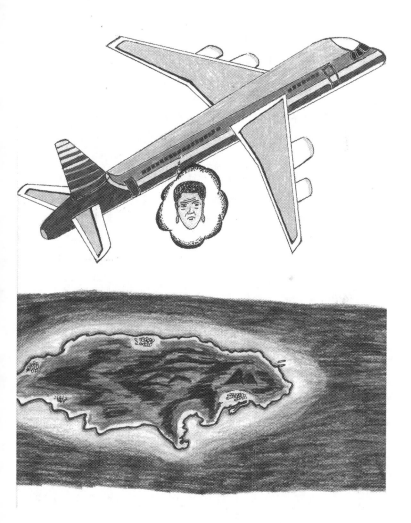

Justine sipped her drink and stared out of the window into the night sky through which they were travelling. What a fool she had been! To pack up—lock, stock, and barrel—and move to the island. Why hadn't she given it a six month or a year's trial period before cutting her ties with England? Instead of selling her flat she could easily have rented it out; now she had no home to go back to. She would have to kotch with her sister until she could arrange to get herself somewhere to live. And another job.

And then there would have to be explanations to her family and friends. What had happened to bring her scurrying back to England after she had left 'for good', full of hope and excitement at the prospect of living in the tropical paradise with her new husband? She had given her sister no explanation when she had phoned and told her that she was coming to the UK and asked if she could stay with her for a few weeks; all she'd said was that she had some business to sort out.

But once she landed in England she would have to give explanations. It would soon become apparent that she was looking for work and somewhere to live, and then everyone would have to know what had brought her back. Then everyone would feel sorry for her. And some would say "I told you so". And she would be talked about behind her back, maybe even laughed at. It didn't bear thinking about.

She drained the glass and waylaid the attendant to get another. If only she could erase the last eighteen months and live them over again. Oh, what a different outcome it would be! Oh, what different decisions she would make!

*

That's when it had all started. Eighteen months ago. Every Saturday morning she would go down to Brixton market to do her week's shopping. She would walk through the market selecting her fruit and vegetables, making sure to buy only Jamaican produce as far as she was able, before going to the supermarket. Then, struggling with the shopping trolley and several carrier bags, she would make her way to the mini-cab office on Electric Avenue.

That particular Saturday morning eighteen months previously was responsible for where she was now. It had been an icy cold February morning and she had been bemoaning the fact that she had to be out at all in such weather. But if she wanted to eat, she had to shop, so she had followed her normal Saturday morning routine. But the icy cold made her rather wish she could live in a country where there was no winter, like Jamaica where she had come from over thirty years ago. She would return there one day, she told herself. As soon as she retired she would return to Jamaica, but retirement was still at least ten years away.

But then a series of events had convinced Justine that fate was giving her a chance to leave England rather sooner than she had planned, and without much conscious thought she had allowed Fate to lead her along on a leash. The sequence of events had started at the minicab office. The cold weather had induced more people than usual to turn to the use of cabs and all the drivers were already out with fares. There were quite a few people waiting and Justine knew it would be a long wait for her turn.

Then Irvin, one of the drivers who carried Justine regularly, had returned to the office and the operator had called out the name of the next passenger on the list. As luck would have it the passenger was going to a destination which was just one street away from where Justine lived, and when Irvin learned this he suggested she let Justine share the cab. The woman had no objections and so Justine, thanking her lucky stars, was spared the ordeal of sitting in the crowded minicab office for the next hour, waiting her turn.

Justine and Irvin had an easy friendship. He was a Jamaican who had come to England less than a year ago to make some money and return home. He had no intention of staying in this icebox, he had told Justine. He had already paid for a piece of land back home and as soon as he had saved a good portion of pounds he was off home to build his house.

After he had dropped off the other passenger he took Justine home and helped her get her shopping up three flights of stairs to her flat, because as usual the lift was out of order. She had invited him to come in for some coffee and he had accepted, although he said he couldn't stay long because the cab office was busy and there was whole heap of money to be made today. She added rum to his coffee and he drank it and left, but not before they had shared a few jokes and had a good laugh.

Justine had been in the process of adding the seasoning to her beef soup later that afternoon when the doorbell rang. To her surprise Irvin had been standing on her doorstep with a bottle of her favourite Chardonnay and a big grin on his face. The smell of the soup was strong in the flat and gave Irvin an opening.

"Mi stay clear down-a cab office and smell yu soup, suh is come me come to beg yu some." His grin was disarming, and Justine, although surprised, had invited him in, glad to have the company since she was single and childless and often lonely for companionship.

They had spent a pleasant afternoon, with Irvin declaring that he didn't know when he had tasted such good soup. Reminded him of his mother's cooking, he said. He told her that he mostly ate 'take-away' because he lived on his own and couldn't be bothered to cook, more time. He said he did not have a girlfriend because his priority was to save as much as possible and he was not going to let any woman 'eat him out'. Justine had been feeling expansive after several glasses of her favourite wine (how had he known that it was her favourite wine?) and had magnanimously invited him to come have Sunday dinner with her the next day.

Later that evening after Irvin had left Justine had wondered why he should have favoured her with a visit when their relationship up to now, although friendly, had been strictly that of driver and passenger. It wasn't as if he was 'looking her'; she was seriously overweight and at least fifteen years his senior; furthermore he had not put any 'question' to her or given any indication that he 'fancied' her. She decided that he was just looking for some home-cooked Jamaican food and someone to socialise with who would not make any financial demands on him.

And she was glad for his friendship and his company, more time. She did not have a lot of friends but kept herself to herself for the most part. After her divorce nearly twenty years ago (her husband had left her because she couldn't conceive) she had felt inadequate and rejected, and had shied away from the opposite sex, finding her comfort in food and liquor. Not that she was an alcoholic, but she found that having a drink helped to stave off the loneliness and helped her to sleep at night.

Over the next few weeks their friendship had grown; Irvin ate at her house regularly and she started baking cakes and sweet potato puddings and preparing special menus for him. Whenever she needed a cab he would carry her, free of charge. They seemed to genuinely enjoy each other's company and their relationship was uncomplicated by sexual issues.

About two months into their new-found friendship Irvin had asked her if she wanted to accompany him to a relative's wedding in Birmingham and she had agreed. She bought new clothes for the first time in years, had her hair and nails done, and even put on a little make-up. She understood that this was not strictly a date, but wanted to look nice so as not to embarrass him.

Irvin had whistled in appreciation when he came to pick her up, and said, "Yu know, Justine, yu's a very beautiful ooman. How come yu nuh have nuh man?" Justine had been flattered, but had responded lightly, "Gwaan! Yu juss a seh suh. Yu nuh si how mi fat an ugly? Nuh man nuh want mi."

"A lie yu-a tell," Irvin had responded. "Any man would be lucky to have yu fi dem ooman. I-man would-a check yu miself if A thought I had a chance, but a classy ooman like yu naa guh want a uneducated mini-cab driver like mi."

Justine hadn't known how to respond; was he taking the piss, or was he genuine? She answered flippantly, "Gwaan yaah; yu mout' too sweet."

But all the way to Birmingham she speculated on the possibilities of a relationship with Irvin. Was he only flattering her, or would he really consider a relationship with her? Despite the age difference? She was forty-nine, and he couldn't be more than thirty-five. *Don't be a fool,* she told herself, but nevertheless a little butterfly flutter of excitement stirred in her stomach. It would be *sooo nice* to have somebody again, after all these lonely years . . .

She had been alone since her divorce. In the early years she had been on a few dates, even had a couple of sexual liaisons, but none had developed into a meaningful relationship. She had gradually lost all confidence in herself and started to become reclusive, seeking solace in food and alcohol. She had a small circle of friends but did not like to socialise, having grown used to her own company and even learned to like it, up to a point. Her friends kept telling her that if she didn't go out she would never meet 'Mr. Right' but she had not been particularly bothered.

But now she suddenly felt the acute loneliness of the preceding years, and looking down into the future she could see nothing but more of the same. *Could* a relationship with Irvin work? Did he really like her, or was he just being kind? The thought of a relationship with a good-looking young man filled her both with anticipatory delight, and with trepidation.

In Birmingham Irvin introduced her to his relatives and friends as ". . . mi good friend, Justine" and she was accepted with friendliness. She even struck up a friendship with one of Irvin's sisters with whom she found she had plenty in common. At the after-reception party, loosened up by several glasses of rum punch, she forgot her inhibitions and danced; she moved gracefully for a woman of her bulk.

Several men asked her to dance and she accepted. She was thrilled when Irvin interrupted a dance and complained that she was supposed to be *his* date. He held her close as they danced, and at one point, for a brief moment he nuzzled her neck, making her so weak with desire that her knees almost buckled.

They had arrived back in London around three in the morning and Justine had been sure that Irvin would ask to stay the rest of the night. She had already made up her mind that she would say yes. He had walked her up to her flat and seen her safely inside, then to her acute disappointment, had said he would see her later for dinner. She hadn't wanted him to leave but she was not brave (or brazen) enough to invite him to stay, so she asked him if he wanted to come in for coffee. He had declined, saying he was tired and just wanted to get to bed. Justine went disappointedly to her own bed.

But she hadn't been able to stop thinking about Irvin and the possibilities of a relationship with him. She began to weave sexual fantasies and create scenarios in her mind. She decided to go on a diet and to start taking more interest in her appearance. She bought new clothes and started visiting the hairdresser and manicurist on a regular basis. When she cooked for him she outdid herself, and supplemented the food with all kinds of home-made juices and Guinness punch thick with Nutriment and spiced with nutmeg and vanilla and a dash of white rum, but took sparingly of these delights herself.

By this time it was early summer and some four months into their friendship, and Irvin had still made no move to further their relationship. Justine started to wonder if he had been making fun of her, watching her efforts at self-improvement and laughing with his friends about it. Perhaps he was just using her to save himself the trouble and expense of providing his own meals. Perhaps he thought her pathetic; to think she could get a man like him . . .

She felt mortified at the thought of being a subject of ridicule at the mini-cab office, and without her realising it her attitude toward Irvin slowly started to change. She found excuses not to be able to cook for him—she was working late, or she was spending the weekend at her sister's or with a friend; she even began using a different mini-cab firm when she needed a taxi. And she started to go out with her friends again.

She did not realise it, but Irvin had noticed her gradual withdrawal from him, and one Monday evening after a Sunday when she had not cooked for him he turned up on her doorstep with flowers and a bottle of Chardonnay. She had just had a bath and was wearing only a dressing gown when she opened the front door. He grinned and said, "A don't know what A do to upset yu, but A come bearing gifts." He proffered the flowers and wine to her.

Justine had missed his company and she was happy to see him. She accepted his offerings and invited him in. Irvin kept pressing her to tell him what he had done to incur her displeasure and she kept denying that she was displeased—only busy, she said. He pouted and told her that he knew she was seeing someone, because he saw how she had lost weight and was paying more attention to her appearance. He professed to be jealous and wanted to know who the man was. "Is him tell yu to stop cook fi mi, doan't?" he demanded.

Justine was delighted at his expressions of jealousy and decided to maintain the fiction of her having a man. "We . . . el . . . him kind-a jealous a way . . ."

Irvin got up from the armchair in which he had been sitting and came and sat beside her on the sofa. He took her hands in his and looked directly into her eyes. "Mi think yu did like mi."

Justine's stomach fluttered and desire washed over her. God! She wanted him! Her need filled her with confusion and made her stutter. "I d . . . did, aahm, I do, but I'm a big woman fi yu . . . I gotta be at least ten years older'n yu . . ."

Irvin was playing with her fingers and massaging the backs of her hands. His touch sent thrills of excitement coursing through her body, and she inadvertently gave a little sigh. Irvin interpreted the unspoken request and leaned over to place his lips on hers, and she gave him no resistance. His hands found their way beneath the dressing gown and caressed her ample breast, and the next thing Justine knew she was naked and the gown was on the floor.

Later they lay in bed and talked about the age difference. It wasn't quite as bad as she had thought—he was thirty-seven to her forty-nine—only twelve years difference; not the fifteen or sixteen she had guessed. He was not at all fazed by the fact that she was twelve years his senior. "It's not like seh mi-a sixteen and you twenty-eight," he said. "The difference not suh big at our age, and anyway I've always preferred bigger women."

"Bigger in age, or bigger in body?" she had challenged. He had cupped her heavy breasts in his hands and weighed them. "Both," he had whispered before kissing them.

Things had happened swiftly after that. Irvin gave up his flat and moved in with her. She was a bit self-conscious about the age difference at first and didn't mention the relationship to her family or friends, but when Irvin surprised her by producing an engagement ring and proposing she knew she would have to come out of the closet and come clean. She gradually began to introduce him into her circle but did not immediately mention the fact that they planned to get married.

Irvin had told her that he had a piece of land in Jamaica and that his reason for being in England was to make enough money to build his house. He had no intention of living in England long term, he had said, so if she decided to marry him she should be prepared to leave England in the not too distant future.

Justine was more than happy to leave England, and told him that she had a substantial savings account which they could utilise to build the house. The only thing, she said, was what would she do for an income out there—she was still several years away from her retirement pension. He said they could buy a bus and a couple of taxis and go into the transportation business, and he also had plans to build a bar and grocery next to the house.

It all sounded viable to her, but when she told her mother and sister they got onto her case big time. "Can't you see that he's just trying to use yu, Justine? Even if you're fool enough to marry him, leave your money in England and let *him* provide for you. And furthermore, I bet he doesn't really have any land; I bet you anything he only wants to marry you to get his stay in England," her sister had said.

Her mother's problem had been the age difference. "Why a young man like that would want a woman your age when whole heap a young gyal out there? Simple—the young gyal dem nuh have nuh money! Justine, yu are a sensible woman; don't mek man turn yu eena eediat."

Justine had been hurt by their words. By inference they were suggesting that he could not want her for herself—did they think that *no-one* wanted her? That she couldn't get a man on her own physical merit? That she had to *purchase* love and affection?

Her friends were just as discouraging. But Justine was the happiest she had been in years, and if her family and friends could not see the change in her and be happy for her, then they could all go to hell. Irvin treated her like a queen, and she had no reason to suspect that he was play-acting. And God! Was the sex good!

They had had a Register office wedding with only her mother and sister and a couple of Irvin's cousins in attendance. The plan was for Irvin to go down to the island and start building the house. They opened a joint account at Victoria Mutual and Justine transferred a substantial amount of cash which Irvin would use to build the house and business place. She had made one concession to the concerns of her mother and sister. Instead of using up her savings she had borrowed against them. She figured that she could make the repayments from her salary until she left, after which she could utilize the income earned from the businesses.

They bought a minibus, and two Lada motor cars to ship down to the island to operate as taxis. Justine was to join Irvin in six months, by which time the house would be liveable and the bus and taxis generating an income. Later, she had sold her flat, left her job, and arrived in Jamaica to live happily ever after.

Except . . .

She was jerked out of her reverie as the plane hit an air pocket and dropped sharply. There were a few "oohs" and exclamations of fright from some of the passengers before it bottomed out and became steady once more. Outside the window it was pitch black—nothing could be seen. She closed her eyes again and returned to her ruminating.

She had bought new furniture to ship down to the island—a new king-sized bed, living room suite with sideboard and dining table, fridge, chest freezer, stove and washing machine. New everything for a new start she told herself. She could afford it—she had lived very frugally and saved the bulk of her salary in various investment portfolios, not to mention the money she got from the sale of her flat. And she deserved it too; she had worked hard for her money; time to enjoy it now.

She had arrived in Jamaica in early December and settled into the house. Irvin had employed a couple of young women to work in the bar and shop and another to help Justine in the house. He had put her in charge of the grocery store while he oversaw the operation of the bar himself. With a bus and two cars on the road, plus the bar and grocery, they enjoyed a good income and Irvin would often take her out on day trips to tour various parts of the island.

Irvin had encouraged her to join the Lions Club and the Returning Residents Association and she soon had a little circle of friends. She settled into a happy existence and began to really enjoy life. Irvin bought her a personal car and encouraged her to go off and explore the island with her friends.

"After all," he said, "you're a lady of leisure now; Karlene can manage the shop without you. Yu work hard all yu life—gwaan guh have some fun now with yu girlfriends."

She was happy. This was the life! She had her hair and nails done regularly, took out a membership at the local gym, dressed nicely all the time and generally lived the life of leisure in a tropical paradise that she had dreamed of. She called her mother and sister to tell them how happy she was and how wrong they had been about Irvin. He was a good husband.

One weekend in May, some five months after her arrival on the island, she had arranged to meet up with friends from the UK who were vacationing in Ocho Rios. She had left early the Friday morning to drive down to St. Ann. She had stopped at the gas station to fill up her tank, only to realise that she had left the wallet with her credit cards in another bag. She had only a minimal amount of cash in hand, and realised that she would have to return home to get them. Irvin's pickup was parked in the driveway and she drove up behind it and exited her vehicle.

As she reached the top of the stairs she thought she heard the helper's voice coming from her bedroom. If the girl was running up her phone-bill she would have words with her, for sure. She knew she could not stop the practice, but she could try and keep it to a minimal level by letting the girl know that money would be deducted from her pay if she was excessive with her use of the phone. And where was Irvin? The girl had a nerve to be using the phone while

Irvin was evidently somewhere around, as his pickup in the driveway testified.

Justine's approach had been silent due to the carpeting on the stairs, and as she reached the bedroom door which was slightly ajar, and was about to push it open she was brought up sharp by what she heard next. Irvin's voice came from the room, clear and sharp, leaving no doubt as to what was being said. Justine paused in her tracks and listened.

"Juss cool nuh man? Mi nuh tell yu seh is you mi love? Be patient, is juss a matter of time, but mi have to mek shi feel nice or else shi wi get suspicious."

Justine's heart dropped like a stone, and her stomach turned over. Sweat broke out on her body, and she felt like fainting. But she shook herself mentally and continued to listen.

"Yu know seh di reason mi guh Inglan' eena di furse place was to set us up. Justine nuh really have nuh say eena nutten—di title fi dis place deh eena my name alone. Har name deh eena di bus and di kyar dem, cause a di two a wi did guh buy dem, but dat's no problem. She kyan get dem if shi want—mi kyan buy more wid di money weh mi a slide weh one-a-way. An' di bar and grocery a do well."

"But suppose shi waan guh court fi di house? Nuh fi har money buil' di house, even dough a fi-yu lan'?" The helper's voice sounded worried. Irvin replied, "Chuh man! Yu worry too much. I man have everything aanda control. Juss trust mi nuh? Mi soon tek care-a Justine."

Was it her imagination, or was there an ominous undertone to the words? Did he intend to kill her, or have her killed? It was not inconceivable. She listened for a while longer until the sounds became amorous, and then she quietly descended the stairs and exited the house. She had no money, but she had a full tank of gas. She would go to Ochi and perhaps she could explain to her friends how she had left her bank cards and borrow some money from one of them. They wouldn't feel any way—they knew she was good for it.

Justine had previously had no idea that she was such a consummate actress. Outwardly she had a wonderful weekend with her girlfriends, and only gave in to her true feelings and tears at night after she had retired to her own room at the hotel. On Monday afternoon she made the return trip home, promising to send the borrowed money by Western Union.

She was full of anxiety about returning to the house. She was sure her presence and eavesdropping had not been detected, and she did not know how she would act with Irvin when she saw him. Should she confront him, or should she act as if she knew nothing? And what about the helper? Should she fire her? But if she did, they would know something was up.

In the end she decided to say and do nothing, but she quietly set about sorting out herself with a view to leaving Irvin. Again she surprised herself with her skill at acting. She treated him normally, only declining to have sex with him, saying she was feeling generally unwell. He acted solicitously toward her but did not press her for sex. She did not fire the helper.

She checked the joint account and found that all but a few thousand dollars had been withdrawn. She drew the balance and closed the account. What a good thing she had kept an individual checking account.

She consulted with a lawyer to see what could be done about getting back the money that had been spent building the house. The news was not good. He told her that it would probably take years in court to sort out and she would have to have irrefutable proof that it was her money which had built it. Did she have receipts for the building material, etc.? She had not. Irvin had been the one who had purchased the material and paid the workmen.

She had all the receipts and the shipping papers for the furnishings she had bought, and she was determined that she would ship every single piece back to England, even if they had to stay in storage until she could get another flat. And no matter how long it took or how much it cost, she was going to fight for the money she had spent building the house, and for the motor vehicles. She would tie him up in court for years, if necessary.

She quickly and quietly went about her preparations. She booked her flight to England and arranged for the shippers to come in the week before she left. She would spend that last week with a friend in Kingston where Irvin would not be able to find her. Everything was going back; bed linen, curtains, and all the beautiful crockery in the cabinets. She notified the police of her intention and showed them her receipts, in case Irvin tried to stop the shippers from packing up the things. She had stopped paying the profits from the grocery store into the joint account and began to let the stock run down.

The day the shipping company arrived to pack up her things she was gratified to see how frantic the helper became when she realised that all the beautiful "Inglan' furniture dem" was about to return from whence they had come.

Cell phones had not yet made their advent and so there was no way of reaching Irvin, who had gone out early in the morning and not yet returned. There was nothing the helper could do.

Only after she had gotten on the plane did Justine allow the emotions to take her over. Only now did she allow the mortification she had felt at Irvin's nefarious plans to wash over her. Looking back, she couldn't believe she had been so strong. No-one had suspected a thing. Irvin had put down her uncommunicativeness to the fact that she was feeling unwell. But he had not suggested she see a doctor. Perhaps he had been hoping that her ailment was serious or even life-threatening.

She had left for Kingston before he returned home. Now, a week later, and thousands of feet above the Atlantic Ocean, she tried to imagine his reaction when he had arrived home to an empty house and a frantic helper/lover. Good thing the loans she had taken had been secured by her investment accounts, which meant that she had been unable to withdraw from them, so although she would have to continue servicing the loans, she still had most of her capital.

She would get over this. Life would go on. But she would never ever again let down her guard where a man was concerned. She had been hurt and let down twice too many times, first by her first husband and now by Irvin. It was not going to happen to her again.

Despite her inner feelings, a little smile of triumph found its way to her lips, and she settled back in her seat and closed her eyes.

12 MARSE DOUGAL'S DILEMMA

Marse Dougal straightened up from the row of callaloo he was weeding, leaned on his hoe, and wiped the sweat from his face with a soiled piece of cloth which had once been a part of Matilda's church dress. He stared at the piece of cloth as he remembered how fond Mattie had been of the dress. It had been given to her by a lady from England for whom she had done 'day's work.' Matilda had been so proud of that dress—she said it made her feel like a queen to wear it—and then Stella had had to go and burn a hole in it with the iron.

Matilda had been so vexed; she had almost killed Stella with beating. The dress had been relegated to 'ole claat' and had found various uses; from duster and furniture polisher, to shoes shiner and sweat rag. Marse Dougal smiled grimly to himself as he remembered.

He brought his mind back to the patch of callaloo he was weeding. He was bone weary; both in body and mind. Sometimes he could hardly see the point in breaking his back and spilling his sweat under the hot sun to wrench a meagre living for himself and Matilda from this dry and ever eroding hillside.

It was no use considering selling the land—it wasn't worth anything to anybody. Most of the topsoil was gone; washed away by the rains because the land had been denuded of trees, and there was nothing to hold the soil in place. The best of the soil now reposed in the rivers and the sea, leaving mainly bedrock.

Most of the young people had drifted down from the hills into Old Harbour. Some had settled in Spanish Town and Kingston, while others had gone to England, Canada, and the USA. Those who remained mostly cultivated and sold ganja. The community now mainly consisted of a few old people who helped each other as best they could.

Marse Dougal sighed in frustrated dejection. If only one of their good-for-nothing children would give them a little financial support—but no, yu bruk yu back fi feed and clothe them, and gi' them likkle schooling, and den dem turn dem back pon yu een-a yu ole age.

Stella had migrated to Kingston, and from there, progressed to the position of Receptionist at one of the North Coast hotels. She was married and had two children. At Christmas time she usually sent a card and photos of the children, and a few dollars. But she never came to visit.

"Oonu live too far off the road, and the children dem not used to pit toilet," she had replied to Matilda's letter begging her to bring the grandchildren for a visit. But at least she kept in touch.

The boys were another matter. It was as if they had dropped off the face of the earth. One by one they had left Country and headed down to the town. None of them had ever written or returned for a visit. Whether they were dead or alive, abroad or in prison, Marse Dougal and Miss Matilda had no idea.

Stella said she had seen Boysie one time in Kingston and he had told her he was looking a visa. She did not know if he had been successful. She had given him her address but he had never written. That had been over fifteen years ago. Of Ivan and Clement, there had been no sight or sound for nearly twenty years.

Marse Dougal sighed again, and turned to make his way back up to the yard. The sun was too hot to do any more work now. He would return in the early evening and weed a few more rows.

As he approached the yard he could hear Matilda singing, *"Jesus is a Rock in a weary land; a shelter in the time of storm."* Every now and then she would intersperse her singing with exclamations of "Hallelujah!" and "Bless yu name, Jesas." She was on the babbeque under the giant ackee tree, beating coffee in a mortar.

As Marse Dougal approached from around the kitchen-side, Matilda ceased her singing, laid down her pestle, and wiped her palms on her ample hips. Her face lit up with the sunny smile that made Marse Dougal remember why he had pursued her so relentlessly sixty years ago.

"Dougal," she said with excitement in her voice, "truly God good to wi. Look 'ere," and she took a letter from under the stone where she had placed it for safekeeping.

Dougal took the letter she handed to him and stared at it. It bore a foreign stamp and postmark. "Yu guh post tiddeh?" he asked Matilda. She shook her head. "Miss Maisie sen' it up wid Marse Lijah."

Marse Dougal slowly drew the letter from the envelope. The signature jumped off the single page at him. Boysie; that good-fi-nutten oldest son of his. What did he want, to be writing them now, twenty years after he had left home?

"Well, what yu t'ink?" Matilda impatiently waited for his reaction. "Uh? What? Wait nuh; A doan't read it yet." He slowly and painstakingly spelled out each word.

"Dear Mamma and Pappa

How oonu do. A bet oonu did tink seh mi dead. Well mi is alive and mi coming home soon. Tek care till mi si oonu.

Boysie.

"Well?" Matilda said again when she judged he had had sufficient time to read it through. Marse Dougal scratched his stubbly grey beard and said sourly, "Is some kine-a trouble 'im get een-a, an' waan come a-bush come hide out; yu mark my words. Twenty 'ears since him gaan an' is now 'im seh 'im-a write? Dis as cheap 'im nevah badda."

Matilda looked deflated. "But Dougal, yu nuh long fi si di bwoy? Fi what-some-evah reason 'im-a come back, mek wi juss gi' God tanks, nuh?"

Marse Dougal sat down on a part of the exposed root of the ackee tree, which had been there since he was a little boy. "Well, 'im kyaan nuh badda expec' mi fi kill nuh fatted calf," he said grumpily. "Beg yu likkle food an' some sugar'n water deh, Mattie."

Matilda went off to the wattle and daub kitchen a few yards from the house to bring his lunch, and Dougal drew water from the rain barrel to wash his hands and face. After he had eaten his lunch he went to lie down for a couple of hours, to rest his weary bones before going back to the callaloo ground.

He had been dozing for a short while when a commotion outside in the yard brought him fully awake. He could hear Matilda shouting; "Oh Glory! T'ank yu Jesas! T'ank yu Laad!" She sounded as if she were laughing and crying all at once. He got up and went to the wooden louvre windows to look out. He saw Matilda being hugged by a tall big boned man. Comprehension was slow in coming; it couldn't be Boysie already; they had only just gotten the letter.

Dougal was tired and reluctant to be disturbed. He relished the thought of some rest before going back to his labours. He shouted through the window at Matilda. "Is what happen to yu, woman? Yu nuh si mi-a try get likkle res' fi guh back a-grung. 'Low mi nuh"

But Matilda could hardly contain her excitement. "But Dougal, yu nuh si seh Boysie come?"

Marse Dougal was not impressed. "'Ow 'im fi come a'ready an' wi juss get letta tiddeh?" Matilda almost screamed, "But him deh-ya. Come si fi yuself."

Marse Dougal, curious despite himself, reluctantly came out of the house. Now at close quarters he could recognise his son. Boysie was taller than he remembered, and had filled out considerably. He looked well-to-do, and sported several gold chains around his neck and a gold watch on his wrist. He wore expensive, well cut clothing and a good pair of shiny leather shoes. He made an impressive figure, which made Marse Dougal feel very insignificant.

Boysie approached Dougal with a big grin, held out his hand and said, "Waapen, Pappa; weh yu-a seh?"

Suddenly Marse Dougal was filled with a blazing anger. The wretched bwoy had been gone for over twenty years, yet here he was greeting his father not only as if he had only seen him yesterday, but also like they were companions! He ignored the outstretched hand, drew himself up to his full height, or as near as his bent old back would allow, and said angrily, "Weh mi-a seh? Weh mi-a seh?

"Mi-a seh yu nuh have nuh mannas, bwoy! Mi-a seh yu wutless an' good fi nutten! Yu mean fi tell mi seh, from yu lef' yah tell now, ovah twenty 'ears, is now yu juss come back? An nevah a line nor a message fi seh yu nuh dead, or fi aaks wi how wi do? Yu know how much yu mumma fret pon yu an yu wutless bredda dem? Yu know hummuch night 'im spen' pon 'im knee a-aaks God fi kip oonu safe? Ef a nevah did fi-har sake, A hood-a run yu weh from yah!"

Dougal only stopped his tirade because he was short of breath and trembling so much he had to sit down. Boysie had not taken this verbal assault lightly. He responded in like anger.

"If it wasn't fi Mamma, I would-a never come back at all! If mi wutless, a yu cause it. When time mi fi deh school, yu have mi a-bush a-work. Chop bush, plant cane, cut cane, climb tree, cut wood, burn coal, tie out goat and cow and donkey. A could-a guh aan and aan. Yu try kill mi wid wuk, and when dat fail, yu try kill mi wid lick. Yu tink mi figgat how yu use to murder mi fi likkle an nutten?!"

Matilda was distraught. "Oonu stap it!" she cried. "Bwoysie, gwaan eena house guh siddung; mi soon come."

Boysie, grumbling to himself, did as she asked. Matilda looked down at Marse Dougal for a moment, and then she said quietly, and with hurt in her voice, "Marse Dougal, mi shame a-yu. How yu mean fi hangle di bwoy suh, after him was away suh long? Mi shame a-yu." And with that she left him, and went inside to join her son.

Marse Dougal was ashamed of himself too. He really was glad to see the boy, and being only human, he couldn't help hoping that Boysie's return would mean some financial aid. He was sorry he had lost his temper like that, and he hoped it wouldn't prevent Boysie from being generous.

Wearily he got to his feet and went into the house. Matilda and Boysie were looking at photographs and laughing. They looked up and stopped laughing as Marse Dougal entered.

Dougal looked straight at Boysie and said, "Bwoy, mi sorry fi how mi carry on likkle while. An mi sorry bout di school an di wuk an di beating dem." He did not wait for a reply, but went dejectedly through the curtain that separated the sitting hall from the bedroom, and sat on the bed with his head in his hands.

He felt, rather than heard, when his son entered the room. He did not look up. He felt the bed sink as Boysie sat down beside him. He heard Boysie sigh.

"Look here, Pappa, mi sorry to'. Mi know seh yu did do the best yu could under the circumstances. Nuff years gone, and nuff water under the bridge." He took out a cigarette, then appeared to think better of it, and replaced it in the pack. He continued to speak, as Marse Dougal had not replied.

"Pappa, A never do too bad a-Foreign. A have some property in Connecticut and a portion a money. A buy piece a road-side land topside here-suh fi yu an Mamma. A gwine put up one likkle house fi oonu."

Marse Dougal raised himself up and took his head from his hands. He gave Boysie his full attention. "Which part a roadside?" he asked with interest.

Boysie caught the note of interest and smiled. "Juss above Nine Mile. Is only one acre, but it flat."

"But one acre a-nuh land. Weh mi kyaan grow pon one acre?"

"Wait nuh? Yu won't have to grow nutten except maybe few vegetable fi oonuself, and dat a only if yu waan to. A going to give oonu a money a month-time suh dat yu kyan stop bruk yu back een-a di sun-hot, and Mamma nuh haffi carry nuh more load guh-a market."

Marse Dougal seemed overwhelmed. His eyes filled, and he said in a choking voice, "God bless yu, Son."

Boysie left soon afterwards, promising to return the next day with his wife and children.

After he left Matilda was so full of excitement that she said she was going over to Marse Lijah and Miss Enid to tell them the news. For once Marse Dougal did not chide her for chatting too much. He was just as excited as she was, but he did not feel the need to go running off to share it with the neighbours. He wanted to be alone to savour the feeling.

Imagine, no more struggling with the ever-steepening hillside. No more getting up before-day, or toiling in the hot sun. Perhaps he could even get some poor fool to buy his ten acres of arid hillside, to supplement whatever money Boysie planned on giving them. Boy, was he looking forward to a life of ease!

And it would be even better for Mattie. No more struggling to market with heavy loads. No more waiting for hours for an overloaded taxi where passengers were packed on top of each other like goods. Maybe they could even pay someone to do the washing and cleaning too. It was high time Mattie relaxed a little. Yes; Matilda's God was finally coming through for her. And not before time; but aftah raall!

A short time later Matilda returned. She seemed a little subdued but Marse Dougal didn't appear to notice. She set about preparing their dinner and after they had eaten and was sitting on the babbeque, she said to her husband, "Marse Dougal, yu know seh is ganja Boysie sell a-Farrin and get rich?"

Marse Dougal sat bolt upright. "What yu saying to mi?"

"Marse Lijah seh him hear Boysie frien' dem a-talk bout it." She looked at her husband. "Marse Dougal, if is true, wi kyaan't tek nutting from Boysie, for dat would mek us as bad as him, and if dat bi di case, den dis as cheap wi did grow and sell ganja fi wi-self.

"A bin serving Jehova God all mi life, and A not gwine start sin now, much less live off-a sin money. And what would Pastah and mi church bredrin dem seh?"

Marse Dougal didn't give two hoots for Pastor and the church brethren. Pastor was alright. He didn't have to work and sweat in the fields. He had his offering money and tithes to live off-of. But he, Dougal, was not going to give up his new-found life of ease just like that. No sir! He didn't exactly approve of how Boysie had come by his money, but like how him done have di money a'ready, well, dem might as well enjoy it.

No sir, he would not be deprived of his well-earned rest from toil, despite Matilda and Pastor. He looked Matilda straight in the eye and said, "A doan't care what Pastah or anybaddy else have fi seh. None a-dem not feeding wi nor buy cloase gi' wi, nor pay wi doctor bill, suh mek dem move and guh-weh!

"Mi son come from Farrin fi provide likkle comfort fi wi een-a wi ole age. If Pastah nuh want wi fi accept wi own-a son charity, well den, mek Pastah provide fi wi!"

Matilda stared at him. She didn't know what to say. Dougal had a point. If they refused Boysie's offer, how would they manage a few years from now when they could no longer help themselves. Would the Lord provide? Isn't that what He was doing now; providing? Or was he merely testing her faith and her convictions? Should she hold her faith, and wait to see if her God would provide an alternative to Boysie's offer?

She did not want to end up depending on the goodwill and charity of her neighbours, and in any case, most of them were in the same position as she and Dougal. Granted, some of them were supported or assisted by their relatives, but most of the young people had left the district.

Apart from all of this, if they refused Boysie's offer, they risked alienating their son all over again. Miss Matilda just did not know what to do.

As for Dougal, although he had made his speech with bravado, he wasn't really comfortable with the knowledge of the source of his comfort. He privately decided to consult Ole Tom, the Spiritualist Healer and 'Reader Man' to get some advice.

The following morning, early, before sunrise, Marse Dougal killed and plucked a fowl and went up to Ole Tom's house a chain up the hill. He offered the fowl in lieu of cash payment, and sat on the chair indicated.

Ole Tom took a pencil and paper and started to read from the Bible. As he read he scribbled unintelligible markings on the paper. Then he started to talk to Dougal.

"Marse Dougal, yu have a dilemma. Is either yu do what mek yu comfortable in *dis* life, and know seh yu will suffer in di afterlife, or else yu bear the suffering, like how our Saviour bear di Cross of Calvary, and know fi sure seh yu wi surely ress in comfort in di bosom of Abraham."

As Marse Dougal left Old Tom and made his way back down the hill he kissed his teeth. He was sorry he had consulted Old Tom; he hadn't helped any; Dougal still had a dilemma. What a waste of a good fowl!

Dougal knew that he would rather be comfortable now in his old age, for after all, how was he to know if there *really was* life after death. But he had lived with Matilda, her God, and her religious philosophy long enough to entertain some suspicion that there might indeed be a Hell to go to after he died. He did not really want to take any chances.

He reached home to find the yard in an uproar. Boysie had returned with his wife and children. The twin boys were thirteen years old, and were excitedly exploring the yard and attempting to climb the old tambrin tree, without much success but with a lot of shouting and laughter. One little girl was about eight years old, while the other was a babe in arms; (currently her grandmother's arms) who was wailing miserably. Marse Dougal was introduced to his daughter-in-law and grandchildren and then he took Boysie aside to confront him about the source of his riches. Boysie looked slightly shamed. "Look here, Pappa; when yu deh a-Foreign yu have to do whatever yu can to mek a living, for nuhbaddy naa gi yu nuh 'bligh.' A admit seh A did sell weed fi a time, yes, but only long enough to get a money fi start a proper business.

"Right now, I have seven record shop between New York and Connecticut, and A promise yu seh A don't sell a stick a-weed fi di last ten years. Suh Mamma kyan tell Pastah and har church bredrin dem seh a record shop mi money come from, if is any a-dem business. Seen?"

Marse Dougal was more than relieved to hear this, and asked Boysie if he had told his mother. Boysie nodded the affirmative. They joined the rest of the family and spent the balance of the day in fun and folic, with Matilda in her element as matriarch of the clan.

As Marse Dougal lay in his bed that night he thankfully reflected that he could look forward to a life of ease with no financial worries, and Matilda was happy to have at least some of her grandchildren around her, albeit temporarily.

Marse Dougal fell asleep with a happy and contented grin on his tired old face.

Marse Dougal's dilemma had been resolved.

13   ONE GOOD TURN

The house was cold and damp. The windows rattled when the wind blew, and little rivulets of water from the condensation ran down and left streaks on the glass, and culminated in dirty little puddles on the rotting window-sills. The wallpaper was peeling from the walls, and the linoleum which covered the floor was old, torn, and dirty.

The old paraffin heater which Eula had tried to clean up gave some vestige of warmth to the bedroom, but the other rooms were freezing cold. And the stench of the paraffin, mingling with stale unwashed bedding and body, permeated the whole house.

The old man, Bill, lay in the bed helpless and fuming. He had been a racist all his life. Every black person was a nigger or a wog, and he hated them all. They had come to his country, taken jobs and housing away from his own people, and now, to cap it all, he had to suffer the indignity of having a nigger in his house taking care of him when his own daughter had abandoned him.

This damned nigger, without being asked, had taken it upon herself to invade the sanctity of his home and taken over, like she had a right. And there was nothing he could do about it. He was too feeble to go out, and the phone had long since been disconnected for non-payment of bill so he couldn't call anybody, always supposing he had anyone to call, which he hadn't.

Eula was Jamaican, and had lived next door to him long enough to know that he was an out and out racist. Indeed, she had often been on the receiving end of his vitriolic insults and name-calling. But now, here she was, taking care of him in the absence of his own daughter. She knew she would have to call Social Services sooner or later. It was quite obvious that Bill's daughter was not coming back. A week had elapsed since the argument, which Eula had heard through the thin walls of the terraced house.

Bill's daughter, Bridgette, had wanted him to sell the house so she could get the money for a down payment on a newer house where she said he would be more comfortable. But Bill was no fool. He knew she was planning to put him into an old people's home; he had overheard a conversation she was having on her mobile phone when she thought he was sleeping.

Well, if she thought he was going to sell his house, she had another think coming. Only over his dead body would she ever get possession of this house, and not even then, if he could help it. He had been born in this very house, and had lived here all his life. Bridgette herself had been born here. Bill intended to die here, and nothing Bridgette could say would change his mind.

Eula had heard Bridgette tell Bill that if he refused to let her put the house on the market, she would move out and leave him to fend for himself. He *had* refused, and as good as her word, she had left. When after two days she still had

not returned, and the milk had not been brought in off the doorstep, Eula had knocked on Bill's door and asked the racist if he needed anything. He had shouted at her through the door, "Get away from my door, you damn nigger. I don't need your help!"

Eula had left him alone.

But the next morning the milkman had noticed the uncollected milk and asked Eula if she knew why it had not been taken in. She explained briefly and the milkman, who had been doing this round for years and knew all his customers, called out to Bill. After an interminable time the old man had managed to get to the front door.

They had been horrified to see his condition. He was weak and emaciated, and getting to the door had taken all his strength. Together they had gotten him back into bed, with him protesting all the while that he did not want that nigger bastard to touch him. The milkman had been embarrassed but Eula had ignored all of Bill's cursing and insults and taken charge. She told the milkman that she would get in touch with Social Services.

There had been no food in the house and the place was damp and cold. Eula had done what she could for him—fed him, and cleaned up the old paraffin heater and bought paraffin so he could keep warm. The only thanks she had received were insults and name calling, but she was a God-fearing Christian woman, and so she ignored them. She had left his front door on the latch so that she could get back in to check on him.

She had been hoping that the daughter would eventually return, but now, a week on, it was obvious that Bridgette had meant what she said. Since leaving she had not once returned to see how her father was doing. Eula could not take Bill on permanently. She would have to call Social Services.

In the event, it was an ambulance she had had to call. That evening she had found Bill unconscious on the floor. He spent a week in the hospital before he died. And still no sign of the daughter, despite police and Social Services searching for her.

Eula was shocked a few weeks later to discover that while in the hospital, Bill had managed to make a Will. Not only had he left the dilapidated old house to her, he also left several hundred pounds in a building society account. He stated adamantly in the Will that not one penny should go to his daughter, but made it clear he was not leaving it to "the nigger" because he had any liking for her, but she had helped him when he needed it, and one good turn deserved another. And in any case, he wanted to teach his daughter a lesson.

Eula didn't give a damn about his reasons. This made up for all the times Bill had called her "wog" and "nigger bastard" over the years. Despite that, she had done the best she could for him, although it must have stuck in his craw to have a nigger bastard being kind to him when his own flesh and blood had abandoned him.

Bridgette eventually turned up to take possession of the house and put it on the market, and nearly had kittens when she discovered that Bill had not only willed it to Eula, but had left her some cash as well. Bridgette threatened to take it to the highest court in the land, but Eula's solicitor said she had nothing to worry about. At Bill's request the Will had been written by a nurse and signed in the presence of several nurses and a doctor who would confirm that he was in full control of his faculties, and had not been coerced.

In fact, Eula had not even visited Bill at the hospital, and had been surprised that he even knew her proper name, since he had never used it, but always referred to her as "wog" or "nigger".

Eula stared contemplatively at the damp, peeling wallpaper, and the old and torn linoleum. The house needed some amount of renovation, but it could be fixed; double glaze the windows, some new wallpaper and paintwork, new lino or carpeting and it would be as good as new. Then she could either sell it or rent it out. She rather thought she might sell it and use the money as down payment on a nicer house in a nicer area and rent out the one she was living in now.

Eula smiled to herself as she remembered Bridgette's face when she had learnt that she was dis-inherited. She did not feel any sympathy for Bridgette. She deserved this. After all, she, Eula, had been the one to take care of Bill in his hour of need, and when all was said and done, as Bill had stated in the Will, one good turn deserved another.

14 THE COOKING AND THE HUGGING

A was fourteen when A went to live with Mamma Dee and Missa Lloyd. Hmmm, A sometimes wonder if them did ever know how close them come to getting rob and kill after them tek me in; A wonder if them ever realise what a chance them was tekking with me?

It was the cooking and the hugging what save them enuh. Mamma Dee cooking was like nothing A ever taste in my life—before, nor since. Bwoy, mi mouth a-water juss to remember them food deh. In the morning time she would-a cook nice juicy liver with nuff gravy and fry dumpling or green banana and yellow yam. Or sometime it would be salt mackerel or stew chicken, or ackee and saltfish.

Then in the evening we would have oxtail and butter-beans cook suh saaf it juss-a drop off-a the bone and melt in yu mouth, and the bone itself pressure so saaf yu could-a chaw it right up. Or sometimes it would be curry goat and white rice, and every Frideh it was fish; and A mean proper sea fish like Snapper and Parrott and Butterfish and Doctor.

Sat'deh she always cook a big pot-a soup, and Sundeh-day time she either bake one whole-a chicken with all kine-a nice thing stuff up inside-a it, or pot-roast one big piece a beef with nuff carrot and dem ting dere. And the amount-a food she put pon mi plate could-a did serve mi and couple-a mi street pal dem fi couple day well, yu zi mi.

And she used to bake nuff to'. Patty and toto; sweet potato and cornmeal pudding, and all kind-a banana and coconut and orange cake. And when she guh Hi-Lo supamarket she buy Buckingham ice cream, and apple and cherry pie from foreign, and one something name lemon merrang pie . . . What a something taste good, man?!

Yes; is the food and the hugging what save dem, for all my intention was to get some-a mi bwoy dem to come rob the house, for some nice things was inside there. TV, radio, video, component set; all computer to'. And Ma Dee and Missa Lloyd did have some nice clothes and shoes and jewellery to'. A good money could-a did mek off-a that house, but when A taste the food the evening, and them tell me that A could stay with them as long as A like, A put off sending fah mi friend-them for a few days, suh A could eat mi belly-full before mi leave.

And then there was the hugging. What a woman love to hug, man? She and Missa Lloyd always a hug and-a kiss-up one anadda; all in front of mi and the other kids them, and nuh feel no way 'bout it. The first time she try hug me, A stiffen right up and hold miself far from her, but she never mek no never-mind 'bout that; every chance she get, she try hug me, or touch mi face, or pat mi pon mi head.

At first A used to draw weh from her, but after a little while A realise seh A like the hugging and kissing; it was just

that A never did have none before, suh A never did realise
how good it mek a one feel. A never like when she pat mi
pon mi head though, for A was'n no dog, yu si weh mi-a
seh, my yute?

Yes, it was the cooking and the hugging what keep me
there suh long. For every time A get ready to guh call mi
bwoy dem fi come deal with di matter, the food hold mi,
and A keep on put it off till after the next meal. And the
hugging was starting to feel real good to', suh A tell miself
that A never have to rush with the robbing, for A could deal
with that anytime . . .

How A come to live with Ma Dee and Missa Lloyd is
like this. A sight them downtown, and A decide to pick
Missa Lloyd, for them did look like them have two shilling,
yu zi mi. But A was'n skill enough dah day-deh, and juss as
A was sliding out the wallet from Missa Lloyd back pocket,
him hold aan pon mi han'.

Well, them call two policeman weh did deh nearby and
them was gwine lock me up, but when A start bawl and tell
them seh is hungry A did hungry, Ma Dee beg fi mi, and
Missa Lloyd look like him always give her what she want,
suh the police warn me, and Ma Dee and Missa Lloyd them
end up carry me guh-a KFC. Ma Dee start ask me all kind-a
question bout mi people-dem, and when she find out seh
is on the street mi-a live, she ask mi if A waan come home
with them.

Missa Lloyd never seem too please, but Ma Dee tell him
seh all A need was some good loving care and attention and
a chance to turn mi life around. A laugh to miself, for all
my intention was to check out them house and see what A
could get to t'ief from them. And Missa Lloyd did know

it to', for when him think A was'n listening A hear him telling Ma Dee that A was too old to learn new ways, and them going regret taking me in, for A was sure to rob and kill them, but Ma Dee was sure that all "the poor bwoy" needed was love.

But it was'n love what hold me at first; it was Ma Dee cooking, and it hold me like how the crack cocaine hold some-a the people dem mi know dung a town.

And another thing to'. I was'n the only one them tek een. Two other bwoy was there, and one likkle girl; all-a dem younger than me, but big people use to come to the house and A get to learn seh is Ma Dee and Missa Lloyd grow them to'. It look like them could'n have nuh pickney fi demself suh dem grow other people own. Is funny how the people weh mek the best parent always never have nuh pickney fi themselves, doah . . . ?

But all of a sudden A find miself with a mother and father, two brothers and a sister, and several aunt, uncle, and cousin. A fine miself with a full belly every day and nice clean clothes fi wear and a nice clean bed to sleep into out of the rain, instead of the cardboard box mi used to sleep under at Hero's Park.

And at night A never have to sleep with one eye open and ready fi get up and run if somebody try to trouble me, for sometimes some of the bigger bwoy them would try to hold down some-a the younger one-dem, to sell to the big man-dem with them big car and fat wallet-dem.

Suh A keep on putting off the robbing, telling myself that A could deal wid dat anytime, and likkle by likkle widout realizing it A become a part-a di family and get suh use to di family life dat A even start to guh school! And widout mi even realizing it di intention to rob just quietly slink weh guh bury itself eena one deep dark hole . . .

*

Dem-a bury Mama Dee todeh. My woman and my two yute-dem never si mi cry yet, but dem si mi cry todeh. A who seh big man doan cry? A lie dem-a tell, my yute.

A gwine miss Mamma Dee y'si. She gi' mi a chance at life, for if A did stay pon the street might-be A would-a dead ahready, like nuff a di bwoy dem mi use to know. Or might-be mi would-a deh a prison. She give mi self-esteem, and teach mi integrity. She show mi what it is to have a loving and supportive family, and mi nuh feel no way fi hug-up and kiss-up my woman in front-a wi pickney dem. And I hug my yute dem all di time, for Mamma Dee cause mi to know what a nice feeling it give.

I juss know seh if nuff more hugging did gwaan, nuff less killing would-a gwaan. Serious ting, my yute.

Bwoy, what a good thing that woman could-a cook, and did love to hug people suh. If it wasn't for the cooking and the hugging, A wonder where in the world I would-a be todeh.

15 VEXTATION

Mi seh, A vex yu si!

A suh bex dat ef yu was to cut mi wid a knife A hooden bleed! No eart'ly 'uman been should-a haffi attallerate such facetiness. But aftah raal!

Wha' dat yu seh? Kaahm dung? *Kaahm dung?!*

Is chew is nat yu dem deh tek libatty wid. Ef di boot did deh pan *fi-yu* foot yu hooden suh quick fi a-tell mi fi kaahm dung! Well, mek A tell yu somet'ing. Yu si di nex' time smaddy try tek libatty wid mi, it naah guh-guh suh, far none-a dem kyaan trace like mi!

Yu si mi? Mi is di Queen a trace. Yes; mi same wan! Yu nuh believe mi? Well mek mi tell yu dis.

A was use to wash fi wan lady dung a Bay, who tek di libatty fi tell mi seh mi spoil up har sinting dem wid di bleach. Is ongle a few of har someting dem did lose likkle colour, an wan or two did patchy-patchy which part di bleach get weh from mi. Oh, an' two piece a har white cloase dem did tun red. Mi did naily figgat 'bout dat.

But hear weh di woman seh to mi nuh. *"A nat paying yu, for yu spwile up my good expensive cloase dem. I gwine fine somebaddy else to wash fah mi; don't bodda comee back."*

148

Well, a get weh wrenk wid har, yu si. A begs to infarm har dat shi have a right fi get smaddy else fi wash har dutty claose dem effen shi waan to, but shi haffi pay mi fi di wuk weh mi do a'ready. Hear di woman nuh, *"Yu have a chice; A kyan pay yu an den sue yu fi mi damage cloase dem, or yu kyan gwaan yu ways an wi squits it out."*

Well, mi couldn' badda wid nuh moah a-di court-house business suh A tell har bout har whats-it-whats-it-nat, an shake aaf har dutty yaad duss aaf-a mi foot an liff up an waak out-a har place. Libatty!

Wan nex' time aggen, wan man employ mi fi wash him cloase an clean him house an cook him food. Di furse time mi cook gi' di man, hear him; *"Di food too salt,"* suh di nex' time a doan use summuch salt.

Mi seh! Yu just kyaan't please some people. Di man tun round an tell mi seh di food too fresh!

Well, A tell him seh is *him* fresh, an since A kyaan't please him none-a-taal, it bess ef him cook him own-a food, an whilse him at it, dis as cheap him clean an wash fi himself to!

Is nuff a dem kine-a libatty deh people try fi tek wid mi, but is chew dem nuh know seh mi is nat a easy smaddy. Mi nuh fraid fi stan up fi mi rights.

An dat brings mi right back to why A suh bex tiddeh-day.

Imagine, A answer di lady advatisement as nice as yu please. "Maaning Mam," A sehs. "A andastans dat yu looking a housekeepa an I come to applicate fah di work . . . .

"Di laas place A work . . . ? Why A leff . . . ? Well, di man weh employ mi, im did too haad fi please, y'si Mam. Im fine fault wid everyting. Ef di food nuh too salt, i' too fresh; A couldn' do anyting right, suh A tells im fi cook it himself, an a waaks out, far mi nuh beholden to nuhbaddy, an mi naah beg dem fi dem wuk!

"Di wan before dat? Well, afta mi bruk mi back a wash di people dem whole-heap a dutty cloase dem, di ooman come tell mi seh shi naah pay mi, far mi spwile up har someting dem wid di bleach. Well fi save miself from tump har dung an en up eena courthouse an jail, A juss waaks weh lef di work.

"But A nevah get fiyah from a work yet; A always leff volunteer. Nuhbaddy kyaan' seh mi evah teef nutten fram dem. Mi hanness an have 'tegrity."

A was sure di lady did-a guh gi' mi di work. It hooda did suit mi juss fine, far is a live-in position, an mi lanlaad eenda rush mi fi di rent weh mi owe him, suh mi did waan mikkase an leff outa deh.

But di ooman neva eena mi a-taal, a-taal.

"Wha' yu seh, Mam? Mi nuh sootable? Afta mi tek two bus an a taxi come suh far? What reason A nat sootable, Mam?

"What yu mean mi in-dite misself? Taak prappa Inglish mek people andastan weh yu deh seh!"

Well fi cut a lang story shaat, di ooman seh mi look like mi have a "hattitude prablem" an dat by mi own-a admission mi kyaan't cook nor wash good. Now, mi aaks yu, mi could-a suh fool-fool fi guh tell smaddy weh mi-a look a work from seh mi kyaan't do di wuk? Wha' kine a eediat dat hood-a mek mi?

Anyways, A did well bex, because is t'ree veekle mi tek fi reach up-a Town an money nuh grow pan tree. Suh a liffs mi head, an pushes out mi chess, an gi' har a good tracing. A tell har seh shi fi eeda stap bleach har face or start bleach har neck to'. A tell har seh har wig nuh siddung good pon har head, an A tell har seh har yeye dem fava toad an har lip dem fava livva. Bi di time A done wid har, yeye-wata a run outa har like a livin stream.

An den a demans dat shi pay mi back mi fare weh mi pay come answa har advatisement, but all di demans A demans, di ooman refuse fi gi mi back mi fare.

Mi seh, A did waan tump har dung, y'si! But mi an Judge an courthouse nuh gree, suh A have to mek up mi mine fi stan di laas.

But A waan tell yu seh it haad fi bear. Ef A neva did suh fraid a courthouse A hood-a tump out mi money out-a har, but mi kyaan tek nuh moah a di courthouse business; no, sah, suh di ongle ting mi kyan do is vex up miself, an swell up wid tempa, an gwaan mi ways.

But A bex yu si!

16 SITUATION VACANT

I had phoned up for the position advertised in the "*Mail.*" It was the ideal position for me; Human Resources Manager conversant with all aspects of Personnel Management, Recruitment and Staff Training. That was me. Good knowledge of Industrial Relations and Disciplinary Procedures. That was me. Experience in staff supervision and assessment. That was me. This was my perfect job and great career advancement.

The receptionist put me through to the Managing Director who proceeded to interview me over the telephone. I wondered why they didn't just mail me out an application form; he would get all the information he needed from that, but I guess he just wanted to ensure that I fulfilled the criteria before wasting time and money sending me a form. I answered his questions and soon began to see the play.

"So, Miss Morgan, what makes you think you can fill our position to our satisfaction?"

"Well, Sir, I meet the criteria in your advertisement; I hold the Certificate of Personnel Management (CPM), for which I received a Distinction. I have the relevant experience, gathered over eight years in the Personnel field, and I come with an abundance of enthusiasm and great innovative ideas for the smoother and more efficient running of your Human Resources Department.

"I am currently employed in Local Government and feel I am now ready to broaden my scope of experience by working within the Private Sector. I am ready, willing, and able to accept the added responsibility that the position in your Company would entail. In short, sir, I am the ideal person to fill your position."

"Well, you certainly *sound* as if you fit the bill. Tell me, Miss Morgan, are you Welsh, by any chance?"

"No, Sir; I'm not," I replied.

"I believe I detect an accent; where exactly are you from, Miss Morgan?"

Well, here we go. The process of trying to determine if I am Black, or White; the main purpose of the telephone interview.

"Well, sir, as a matter of fact, I am from Gloucester, which isn't too far from Wales," I said placidly, "and I guess it is remotely possible that some of my forebears were indeed Welsh."

His manner became slightly more open, (or was it my imagination?) and he asked if I could come for an interview the following day. Of course I said yes. After all, he may not really be another racist; perhaps I was just being over-sensitive.

But then I had every justification for being oversensitive, in my opinion. I had the qualifications to progress further up my career ladder, yet for some reason I was not going anywhere. I had been in my present position for three and a half years, and it was time to make a move before I stagnated. I knew I was good at my job; it showed both in results and in verbal recognition from my Senior Officers, so why was I not progressing when my white colleagues, some of them not as able and efficient as I, were being promoted, or obtaining jobs in the Private Sector?

I have never had a 'chip on my shoulders'; never felt that anything that happened to me was a direct result of my being black. Granted, I had had to work harder than my white colleagues to gain the same amount of recognition, but that is an undisputed fact of life when you are black in a white society.

I had reached my present position by working my way up through the Department; first as Clerical Assistant, then Senior Clerical, through Personnel Assistant, till I achieved the position of Personnel and Training Officer. It had taken me eight years, and now I was ready for further challenges. Since I was unable to advance within the scope of my present employment I was prepared to move to the Private Sector. But after numerous interviews which, from my point of view, seemed to go well, I still had not secured a position. I reluctantly concluded that my ethnic origin must be a significant factor.

My interview was for eleven o'clock the next day. I woke early, had a long soak in a 'Fenjal' bath, and washed my hair. I manicured my nails and creamed my skin until it positively glowed. I felt good. I took my time and dressed with extreme care. Then I caught my dreadlocks into a hairnet, (which makes me look quite sophisticated, I think) and I was ready.

The Company was situated at London Bridge, and I wasn't sure about parking facilities, but I decided to drive, anyway, rather than take the underground. I arrived at ten-thirty, and was fortunate enough to find an empty parking metre almost immediately. Now, *that was* a stroke of luck. I punched in five twenty pence pieces, and leisurely made my way into the building.

I made myself known to the Receptionist who told me to take a seat and complete the application form while she advised the Managing Director that I had arrived. While I waited, having completed the form, I examined my surroundings. It was one of the major construction companies, and displayed around the Reception area were models of buildings for which they had won awards. On the walls, too, were certificates of achievement—this company was big and successful; one could go places working with them.

At five minutes past eleven a smartly dressed man, whom I assumed to be the Managing Director, walked into the Reception. He gave me a cursory glance and looked around in a slightly bemused manner.

I wasn't mistaken. About his racism, I mean. He looked at me with ill-concealed shock and asked, while still searching with his eyes for the white girl from Gloucester with the possibility of Welsh forbears, "*Miss Morgan?*"

I stood up and extended my hand. "Good morning, sir," I said pleasantly. "You must be Mr Sanderson?"

He, very reluctantly I thought, shook my hand. "Yes. Yes, I am. Please come into my office." *Come into my parlour, said the spider to the fly . . .* His voice was not at all inviting.

He told me to take a seat, and placed himself behind his large untidy desk. *How I would love to tidy that desk!* He sat there looking at me for several seconds, and then he said accusingly, "I thought you said you were from Colchester, with Welsh grandparents? You are obviously from either Africa or the West Indies."

Oh, how I hate grown men who pout! But gone were the days when a prospective employer could tell by one's voice on the phone whether one was 'acceptable' by virtue of race or nationality for any given position. I almost felt sorry for the sorry specimen of a man—almost, but not quite. I answered him.

"No, sir; you are mistaken. I am not from either Africa or the West Indies, although my *parents* were born in Jamaica. But I am as British as you are; I was born in *Gloucester*, not *Colchester*, and I was only speculating on the possibility of Welsh forebears, given that Morgan is a Welsh-derived name." I spoke mildly. "Does the fact that I am black affect my eligibility for the position?"

There was no challenge in my voice, but he began blustering as if I had threatened to report him to the Race Relations Board. "NO! No, of course not, but you really *sounded* quite white on the telephone."

"Really?" I asked, in a mild conversational tone, "and how exactly does *white* sound? Please forgive my ignorance, and enlighten me."

I spoke gently, but inside I was boiling, and I knew my eyes were flashing fire. He must be inordinately aware that I was not pleased.

"Well, you know what I mean . . . ," he began, but I cut him short. "No sir, I don't know what you mean; however, since my being black does *not* negate my application, perhaps we could proceed with the interview?"

"Of course; of course."

By now I suspected that he was fully aware of the extent of my annoyance, but I did not care. No job was worth the erosion of my self-esteem and dignity. He probably had no intention of offering me the job, anyway, but he had to go through the motions of the interview, since I was already here.

He began to tell me about the position. It was for a Human Resources Manager who would be entirely responsible for policy, procedures, and the smooth running of the Human Resources Department. It seemed to me that Mr Sanderson emphasized the negative aspects of the job.

"The position is a highly stressed one with constant worries about meeting deadlines. In addition, the three thousand plus workforce is predominantly male, and mostly aggressive and undisciplined. Absentee levels are high and timekeeping is casual.

"The successful applicant will need to be of forceful character; not someone who would be easily intimidated, or offended by the aggressive behaviour and language of these construction workers, who, as a matter of course, regularly use swear words, which we term 'building language.' In addition, attendance at evening and weekend meetings would be an integral part of the job. Shall I go on?"

Oh, so you want to put me off the job? Well, not on your life, mate! I am most certainly not going to make it easy for you.

"Well, you know, sir, I have worked in highly stressed situations; in fact I perform at my best in a crisis. Meeting

159

deadlines is simply a matter of good organisation and communication, and of course, good support staff.

"Attending unscheduled meetings is something one expects at this level and something I am well used to. I have no objections, as long as I am adequately compensated for my time, either by way of overtime payments or time off in lieu.

"As for the undisciplined workforce, if you do not have a Disciplinary Procedure in place I can devise and implement one. If you already have one, I can begin to enforce it, with support and cooperation from Line and Senior Managers."

"Yes, yes. Well, we do have other applicants to interview, of course, but you will be hearing from us in due course. (*Don't call us—we'll call you . . .*) I was being dismissed. I decided to fire a parting volley.

"And by the way, Mr Sanderson, it is *quite conceivable* that I might have Welsh blood running through my veins; after all, the white colonialist slave system gave carte blanche for you white slave-masters to rape my African ancestors with impunity, so mixing your blood with ours!"

There! That was it. I definitely would not get the job now.

But I walked out of that office with my head held high, and my self-esteem and dignity intact.

17 THE GOOD BOY

Miss Elsa was weary. She had been downtown from morning and had sold only one jeans skirt, a few panties and a brassiere. She owed rent, and exam fees, and there was no food in the house. She had used up the little money to re-stock her stall, but sales were not going well—everybody was feeling the pinch. And part of the problem was that everybody was selling the same things.

Her stomach grumbled and she rubbed it, dislodging a huge belch which erupted into a loud growl. Gas was taking her up. The little cornmeal this morning had been just enough for two cups of porridge for the girls, and they had to have it half-sweetened because the condensed milk was finished and there was barely a spoonful of sugar in the pan. Her stomach growled again. She was going to have to buy a cup of soup and a patty.

She hated to dip into the little money, but she had to eat. She couldn't afford to drop down, or what would happen to the girls? Shanelle was doing good; she would be taking GSAT this year, and Shanique was doing her CXC. Six subjects. Miss Elsa didn't know yet where the money was going to come from to pay the exam fees, but she would find it from somewhere, because she was determined to see her girls elevate themselves from the ghetto, and maybe elevate her too along with them. She was so proud of her girls.

Her son Roland had left home from he was seventeen. He hadn't done too well in school mostly because he had to miss it so often for lack of funds, but things had been a little easier with the girls because of his help. He had gotten a job at the wharf and every week he would put a couple of thousand dollars into Miss Elsa's hands. She had wondered how he could afford to give her so much but he had brushed it off, saying his job paid good and there was 'hustling' too. She hadn't pursued it; he had always been a good boy.

But not anymore. Because *he* was no more. Roland couldn't help her anymore—because Roland was dead. Dead—and it was all her fault. If only she had done *something* about her discovery . . .

Her stomach growled again, and she took some money from the precious store and got up from her stool. "Babsy, A going to buy one patty an' a cup-a soup. Yu waant anyting?" Babsy didn't. "Ahright den; soon come." She didn't have to ask Babsy to watch her stall and take care of any customers who happened by—it went without saying.

She returned a short while later with the food and sat down behind her stall to eat it. As she ate, her mind returned to Roland. She remembered how he used to love patties as a little boy—how eagerly he would await her arrival home from town to see if she had brought him one that day.

He had been a good boy; mannersable and helpful around the place. By the time he was twelve he was helping her out financially and when she asked him where him getting money from he said he and a friend were cleaning people yard and cutting them grass. Sometimes he had come home with meat and tinned food and fruit and vegetables which he said people whose yard he cleaned had given him. Elsa accepted them gratefully without any doubts as to the veracity of Roland's words. Even after he had left home he continued to supplement their larder and income, and Elsa thanked God for such a dutiful son.

She conveyed a plastic spoonful of chicken foot to her mouth and sucked the bones clean before chewing them up and spitting them onto the cover of the soup cup. She didn't like to think about the situation—Roland was dead and buried—but somehow her mind kept going back over and over the events leading up to his death. Would he still be alive if she had acted differently? Was it her fault her son was dead?

Roland had been living away from home for over five years, but two weeks before his death he had come to the house in the small hours of a Sunday morning with some things in a scandal bag. He said that he and his baby-mother catch a-fight and they both needed space to cool out for a couple-a days. Miss Elsa was always happy to see her bwoy and so she gladly welcomed him.

Roland had remained in the house for one week straight, saying he was depressed and didn't feel like going to work or seeing anyone. He assured Miss Elsa that he would not lose his job as he had spoken to the Baass. By Friday evening he evidently felt better because he dressed and went out, and had not returned that night. Miss Elsa didn't see him again till Monday evening, and she supposed he had made up with his baby-mother and had returned to his home.

But on the Sunday, prior to his return on Monday evening, Miss Elsa had made a horrific discovery. When they were younger all three children had slept in the same room, but since Roland had come home temporarily Miss Elsa had given him her room and slept in the girls' room on the single bed that used to be Roland's. On Sunday morning she had gone into her own room to strip the bed and put fresh sheets on as a prelude to returning, since Roland seemed to have resolved his differences with his girlfriend.

She stripped the bed and put the sheets to soak in a wash-pan. Then she returned to the room which she dusted and swept. Finally she decided to turn over the mattress since this side was getting lumpy and the springs were beginning to come through. She gripped the mattress firmly in her two hands and pulled it toward her slightly, before easing it up so she could lean it against the wall where she would be able to grip the bottom and pull it so that it would fall over onto the other side. As she lifted, she noticed a black scandal bag right in the middle of the bedstead and wondered briefly what it was doing there. She knew she had not put it there, so Roland must have put something there for safekeeping.

She'd had no premonition of danger or of anything being out of the ordinary, but only wondered what was in the bag and why he felt he had to go to such lengths to safeguard it. When she reached for it her hand encountered something hard, and when she picked it up it presented a solid weight in her hand. She put her hand inside the bag and withdrew the object which was wrapped in a brown and white ganzie. Even then she felt nothing untoward, but only an idle curiosity. She unwrapped it from the ganzie . . .

. . . And nearly drop down same place . . .

For in her hand was a gun, and she suddenly realised to her horror that the ganzie was not brown and white at all—it was white, all right, but the brown parts were dried blood . . . !

She had dropped them both and run out of the room, but she immediately realised that she would have to put them back, loath as she was to touch the objects—not even wanting to look at them. But she forced herself to return to the room and wrap up back the gun in the blood-encrusted ganzie and replace them in the bag and under the mattress. She remade the bed as quickly as she could and left the room.

For the rest of the day her mind worried and fretted over her discovery. Where had Roland got the gun, or more to the point, what was he doing, or worse, had done, with it? Whose blood was on the ganzie? Roland didn't have any injuries that she could see . . .

What should she do about her discovery? Should she tackle him about it? She cast her mind back to the previous weekend to see if she could remember any news reports of shootings over the Saturday night/Sunday morning when Roland had turned up in the before-day morning with a story about falling out with his girlfriend. She couldn't remember specifically, but there were always news reports of shootings, anyway.

Should she encourage him to turn in the gun? But that would mean turning himself in, or at the very least giving a credible story as to how he came by the weapon. Maybe he could say he found it, or maybe he could just leave it somewhere and call the police anonymously and tell them where it was. *But what was Roland even doing with a gun . . . ?*

Elsa didn't know what to do about the girls, but she didn't want them in the house with the gun. Luckily they were at church with their grandmother, but when they came home and had eaten their dinner she would let them take their school things and go and kotch with their granny for a few days until she get this thing sort out.

She tried calling Roland's cell phone to tell him that she wanted to talk to him but it kept going to voicemail. She didn't usually leave messages, but after several un-answered calls, she finally left one telling him that she needed to talk to him urgently. Still it wasn't till the Monday evening that Roland had returned to the house and Miss Elsa, with a great deal of trepidation but as much determination, had brought up the subject of the gun and the bloodstained ganzie.

Roland had looked angry for a moment, a look Miss Elsa had never seen on his face before, but then he had fixed his face and said, "Mamma, is nutten fi yu concern yuself bout; mi juss a secure it fi a frien', yu zi mi."

"How yu mean nutten fi concern miself about? Yu bring gun come eena mi house and come-a tell mi foolinish. Suppose yu bring down police and soldja pon wi inside here, fi come shoot up mi and yu sista-dem?" Roland had replied calmly, "Mamma, dis-a di laass place dem hood-a look. Nuhbaddy hood-a evah expeck fi fine a gun yassuh amongx good people like yu."

Miss Elsa had not been mollified. "But why yu haf to keep it *here*? To put mi and yu sistah-dem eena danger? And who-fah blood deh pon di ganzie?" But Roland had told her sternly that the less she knew the better.

She had never seen this side of her son. This was a side that she did not like—one that she feared. What had happened to her loving, caring son, Roland? Who was this stranger? Despite her new-found fear of her son she demanded, "Yu get those things out of this house right now Roland! Dem an mi not staying inside here, yu anderstan' mi?"

Roland had not been daunted. "Right here is di safest place fi dem right now, Mamma. Stap fret yuself cause everything cool, everything aanda control. Juss couple more days and dem out-a here, yu zi mi." He spoke like he had no intention of carrying out her wishes. Miss Elsa had become angry and raised her voice. "Roland, get those t'ings out of mi house right now or A will call the police and ask them to come tek them weh."

Roland's face had become so dark and angry that she had taken an involuntary step backwards away from him. He had grabbed her hands and thrust his face down into hers and snarled, "Mamma, mek mi tell yu sumt'ing . . . yu need to pretend seh yu nevah did guh faas with what nuh concern yu, yu hear? Yu need to fahget seh yu evah si anyt'ing and juss gwaan bout yu business as usual and stop talk foolishness bout police. Is kill yu waan dem kill mi?"

Miss Elsa had stared at this stranger who was her son, and had not known him. He filled her with terror. She was afraid to have the gun in the house, but she was more afraid to do anything about it. After Roland had left the house again she had looked under the mattress hopefully. But the scandal bag was still in place.

For the next few days Miss Elsa had lived in terror. She had instructed the girls to remain at their grandmother's and not to come to the house until she sent for them. She didn't know what to do. Should she call the police? No, the risk was too great—somehow it would get out that she was an informer and that would not only put her in danger, but her entire family. She couldn't do it; she had her girls to think bout.

She thought of taking the scandal bag and dumping it somewhere, but she was afraid of what Roland would do, and in any case if the gun was not returned to the owner she knew what the consequences would be. The same as if she informed. She had believed him when he said the gun belonged to a friend—she could not—did not want to believe—that it belonged to Roland.

Two days later he had returned to the house again and when he left this time the bag was gone. Miss Elsa had breathed a hefty sigh of relief, which was quickly replaced by the fear that the gun might be going to "work" and that Roland would again bring it back for safekeeping afterwards. She had no doubt that it was a working tool— the bloodstained ganzie could testify to that.

Miss Elsa made sure to listen to every newscast. There were various reports of gang-related shootings, some in Town, and some in the country. There were reports of shootouts with the police, and of gunmen getting killed. She listened fearfully for the names but did not hear her son mentioned. She called his cell phone but when he answered, she hung up. She only wanted to make sure he was alive.

Thursday and Friday came and went and Roland had not returned with the gun. Miss Elsa began to breathe a little easier. She was thinking that if the weekend passed without incident the girls could come home; they had been very curious as to why they were not allowed to come to their house, but their mother had been adamant in her instructions without giving them any explanation. They were good girls; they did as they were told.

Miss Elsa had never seen her son alive again. On Saturday she was downtown at her clothing stall when her cell phone rang. Without preamble a voice had shouted into her ear causing her to hold the phone at a distance. At first she had not heard what the person said, and then it had hit her, causing her to drop the phone and bawl out in loud anguish before dropping down in a dead faint.

She had lived through the aftermath in a daze. There had been a demonstration. The community cried foul and accused the police of murdering an innocent, kind and hardworking man, who was a loving and generous son and brother. Shanique appeared on TV in great distress, crying, "Murdah! Dem murdah mi bredda! Mi bredda wassen no gunman. How mi gwine guh school now? How mi gwine pay mi exam fee now? WI WAAN JUSTICE!"

And Miss Elsa could say nothing. Could do nothing. It was all her fault. She should have gotten rid of that gun. Should have called a lawyer and taken both Roland and the gun in. If she had, he might still be alive. Prison was better than death. It was all her fault.

She went about the funeral arrangements on autopilot. She had nothing to say when people wanted to discuss the situation. They did not press her; the woman was obviously in deep grief over the murdering of her son by the police. Everyone could understand that. He hadn't deserved that— why the police don't guh look for real criminal and gunman and stop murder innocent people pickney. Roland had been a good bwoy . . .

"How much fah dah jeans pants deh?" A voice brought Miss Elsa out of her reverie. Two women were standing in front of the stall examining the goods. She pushed herself up from the stool, wiped her hands on her hips and gave the customers her full attention. There was nothing she could do for Roland now, but she still had her girls to think about. She badly needed a sale.

She put on her best smile and proceeded to secure her sale.

18 REMINISCENCES

Where 'old man's beard' used to grow, houses now stand. Where foxgloves and harebells used to tussle with the blood red poppies, lettuce and cabbages now sit in sedate orderly rows. Where woodbine and dog roses once wrestled to entwine themselves upon the hedgerows and oak trees, neat privet hedges now prohibit their very existence. Oh, how I miss the Gloucestershire of my youth!

Oh no! The old hollow oak tree is gone! How we loved to play inside that old hollow tree. We kept a store of food in the bole, often to find that the squirrels, or the ants, or both, had gotten to it before we returned to claim it. It was a large and spacious hollow in which we kept all manner of treasures. Our friend, whom we had christened "Mr Long Neck Man," because we did not know his name, and because his neck was so long and skinny, told us that the tree must be at least a thousand years old, and must have been planted by Robin Hood when he came to visit Gloucester from Sherwood Forest in Nottingham, an event he claimed to remember well.

Mr Long Neck Man! Where on earth did I dredge *that* memory up from? I remember that some of the boys used

to call him "Giraffe Neck" but we girls always called him "Mr Long Neck Man." He used to buy us sweets, and ice lollies, and ice cream cones; and we took them, ignoring our parents' warnings about taking things from strangers.

But to us he wasn't a stranger. He lived in our community and our parents saw him every day as he came and went about his business. He used to sit in the field with us, and tell us stories about Brer Fox and Brer Rabbit, about Sinbad and the Arabian Nights, and about Robin Hood and his Merry Men. He claimed to have been a participant in all of these adventures, and gullible little kids as we were, we believed him. He kept us enthralled for hours.

We taught him how to make daisy chains, and he taught us to make corn-husk dolls. He knew *everything*; the names of all the trees and flowers and birds and animals. He knew the names of the different variety of moths and butterflies flitting here and there, their translucent wings catching the sunlight. He told us how we could tell the age of a tree by counting the rings in its trunk. Of course we would first have to cut down the tree . . .

He always gave us his full attention, and never got tired of us pestering him with our myriad questions. He was our friend, and we loved him in our childish ways. We used to pick blackberries and crab apples for him, and even "scrogged" (stole) apples, plums and pears from people's gardens and orchards to give to him.

Of course he never knew that they were stolen property; but then we did not consider "scrogging" to be stealing; it was an integral part of country childhood life. And in any case, we were only doing what Robin Hood did; taking from the rich to feed the poor—the poor being our friend,

Mr Long Neck Man. He was so skinny; he really needed fattening up.

He lived totally alone in the big house standing in its own grounds at the end of the lane. We never saw anyone else enter or leave that house, and we wondered if he actually ate. My, but he was skinny!

And then, one languid summer, he disappeared. Just disappeared. It was in the middle of the summer holidays, and it was too hot and humid to do anything more than just languish lazily under our tree. One day he was telling us (again) the story of the Pied Piper of Hamelin—leaving it at a most exciting part, to be continued next day—but next day, well, he just wasn't there.

This was most unusual; he had never missed a day of our holidays before. After two days we thought he might be sick, or something, so we asked our parents if we could go and knock his door to find out. Denise's Mum was concerned, and came with us. We knocked, but got no reply. Denise's Mum said maybe he had gone to visit relatives, but we knew he would have told us if he planned to go away. He was our friend; he would not just leave without telling us.

My brother said maybe he was lying dead inside and that we should break in and find out, and the rest of us turned on him and nearly killed him in our indignation at his morbidness. Denise's Mum said we should ask the local constable to make some inquiries if we were really worried. We were, so off we trotted to the community police post.

Constable Jenkins was also our friend. He greeted us with the words, "Hi-ya, kids; heard about your friend, Mr Long Neck Man, then?"

"No," we chorused. "We can't find him anywhere, and we're worried. Do you know where he is?"

"I most certainly do. By this time I expect he is safely ensconced on remand while he awaits his trial. I expect in a few months he will be taking up residence in Her Majesty's Prison at Dartmoor."

We gasped in unified horror. Prison! Trial! Why? What did he do? It must be a mistake. Not *our* Mr Long Neck Man! We made such an almighty racket in that Gloucestershire police sub-station, that Postie, the postman, passing by on his bicycle, stopped to see what the ruckus was all about.

It turned out that our friend had been making counterfeit money in the back room of his big empty house. There was a large garden at the back of the house, and then a field, so that it was not likely that anyone would hear the grind and clatter of the printing press. But one night a tramp had been sleeping under a hedgerow at the edge of the field near to the garden. He had heard the press in the dead of night, and thinking the house haunted, had fled. Encountering Constable Jenkins doing a night round, he had persuaded him to come and listen to "the 'ghosties' in the big house."

The constable had listened, and then grim-faced, had radioed for his sergeant. Together they had gone into the house, and in the middle of the night, carted away Mr Long Neck Man.

That was twenty-odd years ago. I wonder how long he eventually spent in prison. I must go and see if the house is still there . . .

There it is; standing stark and silent against the sky. It looks unlived in, still. After our friend had gone, men had arrived and moved out some things, before boarding up the house. After a while we had bored a hole in the fence and the garden had become our next favourite haunt, next to the old hollow tree.

The house looks incongruous, standing there in isolated misery at the end of the lane, in a tangle of weeds and undisciplined vegetation, and surrounded now by modern bungalows and maisonettes, each boasting neat pocket-handkerchief lawns or vegetable patches.

Oh! But look! There, in the overgrown garden, and all along the broken fencing . . . The missing old man's beard, the harebells, and the woodbine! Some tangible memories of my childhood are still here, amongst the poppies and the memories.

Pity about the old hollow oak tree, though . . .

Let me go down the road a little, and look at the maisonette we used to live in. Ah, there it is. It looks the same; older, and needing a fresh coat of paint, but easily recognisable. The avenue looks the same, only somewhat smaller than I remember. The village green is still there, separating the shops and private houses from the Council flats.

There's the playground with the swing that I fell off of . . . I cut my knee rather badly, I remember. And the slide. I still wear proudly the scars just below both knees, where I constantly knocked my legs against the slide's metal ladder on the way to the top. We used to wax the slide with furniture polish for a faster descent, and we would often be unable to brake at the end, and go flying off onto the grass which was mercifully thick and springy.

I'm glad to see that the "conker" or horse-chestnut tree is still there outside the playground fence. It provided conkers by the hundred, and the boys had made a swing which was far more exciting than the swings in the playground proper. An old tyre was suspended by a rope from a magnificent branch of the tree and provided a much higher and more fearful swing. One had to climb onto the playground fence to get access to the tyre, so none of the smaller children could use it, which was just as well. Michael broke his leg falling from it, and we were banned from using it again.

Let me walk down here and reminisce a little more. There's the little lane leading to the back of the gas works . . . Aah, and there's the little brook with the woods on the other side. Thank God they didn't demolish that to make way for houses. The brook is a very narrow one. I jump across. Crab apples grow in profusion here. I pick one and bite into its tart sharpness. Urgh! Some things remain the same. The woods are full of bluebells and violets and mushrooms. Or perhaps they're toadstools. Who knows, or even cares? I would deign to eat neither.

Guess it wouldn't be right not to visit my old school. I'll have to cross the busy main road where Gillian's sister, Carrie, got killed. That was a totally unnecessary accident; I had realised that, even at my tender age. Why had she not used the pedestrian bridge which was there so that we did not have to face the volume of traffic on the Cole Avenue? We would never know; no-one got the chance to ask her; she was hit by a bread van and killed instantly.

Our parents hardly allowed us to forget Carrie in their constant admonitions for us to use the bridge at all times. I needed no such admonition. *I* was taking no chances with the Cole Avenue.

There it is; the bridge. Had a recent coat of paint, I see. Still looks solid and sturdy. I used to imagine what would happen if it suddenly collapsed while I was crossing; would the weight of it crush the cars we fell on, or would I end up underneath as a flattened out version of me? Then there was always the possibility that I would be thrown clear only to break every bone in my body, or to be run over by a bread van. No matter which way I looked at it, if it did collapse with me I didn't stand a chance of getting out alive and in one piece. But, particularly bearing Carrie in mind, I preferred to take my chances with the bridge, as opposed to the Cole Avenue.

Aha! My first British school. Aahh! The memories! Good and bad. Gosh; would you believe it looks exactly the same? Except . . . wait; the playground looks *so* much smaller. In fact the whole school looks smaller; look at the bicycle shed—was it really that small?

I remember well my first day here. Seven years old and lately arrived from Jamaica. I was being thrust among white children for the very first time in my life. *I* could understand *them* well enough, but they seemed to have difficulty understanding me.

I understood very well when they called me "nigger" and "gollywog" and "monkey". I didn't know what those things were but I recognised the tone as being insulting and derogatory. I promptly began to thrash the living daylights out of Ashley Warren who was the leader of the pack, until the teacher pulled me off.

She called me a "little 'she-devil'" and made me stand under the clock in the corridor for the rest of playtime. When class reconvened she thought she would humiliate me by making me read aloud in front of the class, "to see if you can read as well as you can fight," she had said.

To her immense disappointment I read the entire passage from *Alice in Wonderland* fluently and without a single wrong word. How was she to know that I could read long before I set foot on English soil; long before I even started school? How was she to know that I had spent hours with my great-grandmother, who taught me herself, reading books sent to me from my parents in England? She wasn't to know. Later I had overheard her telling another teacher that ". . . she reads very well for someone from Jamaica, but we'll have to watch her temper . . ."

No-one had made any attempt to find out what the fight had been about. I had been immediately branded as the guilty party, and was ostracised by the rest of the class. One girl named Cheryl decided to throw caution to the wind and befriend me, and was promptly "sent to Coventry" for her trouble. This meant that no-one was allowed to speak to her. She, just as promptly, gave in and left me to my isolation in "Coventy".

It did not last long, however. They were naturally curious about me, not having had any direct contact with a black person before in their short lives. The mass exodus of Jamaican children to join their parents in Britain was just beginning, and it was still a novelty for many white children to be near, or even to speak to, a black person. Indeed, many of them were afraid of us, and scampered away or held onto their parents for dear life if we approached too closely. But my classmates could not contain their curiosity for long, and little by little they started asked me questions.

Where was Jamaica? Did any white people live there, or only blacks? Did my colour come off when I had a bath? If they touched me, would the colour come off on their hands?

I became a minor celebrity when it was discovered that I had actually flown in an aeroplane, and I had to tell them what it felt like. Of course I did not tell them that I had gotten air-sick and vomited all over my blue taffeta dress.

Should I go in? What for? It's over twenty years since you went to school here, for heaven sakes. No one is likely to still be here who remembers you. All your old teachers must be dead and gone, or at the very least long since retired. *Nonsense; twenty years isn't all that long. People don't move much in these country towns; one of the younger teachers might still be here.*

Hesitantly, the main door. To my left, just inside the door, the Headmaster's office. To the right along the corridor leading to the dining hall, the Secretary's office. I knock, and a voice bid me enter. I walk in.

"Hello; I'm sorry to trouble you, but I used to attend this school as a child and I just wanted to see it again before I leave England to go home to Jamaica. This place has a lot of memories for me. Do you suppose you might ask the Head if I might walk through the school?"

There. That wasn't hard, was it? I am summoned to the Head's office in response to the Secretary's phone call. What a pleasant man. He is asking me the years of my attendance at the school. I tell him. "Oh," he says, peering into my face. "My father was Head here during that time. As a matter of fact I used to come here myself as a boy. If I remember correctly, Mrs Anderson was here during your time . . ."

"Mrs Anderson?" I ask him. "I don't recall a teacher of that name . . . ?"

"Oh, she would still have been 'Miss Fishpoole' at that time. She married and became Mrs Anderson."

Miss Fishpoole! Yes, I remember her. I was in her class in the First Year. She who had called me a 'she-devil'. Is she still here? And fancy the Head being my old Headmaster's son . . .

He offers to take me around the school. I go into all my old classrooms. I give a talk to the children about the school in my day. They applaud when I finish. I feel like a celebrity. I am taken into the Staff room and given tea and scones. Miss Fishpoole, now Mrs. Anderson, comes breezing in. The years have not been kind to her. She is blotchy and obese.

"Hello. It's always nice to see one of our old pupils. Which one are you . . . ? Claudine Rhone . . . ? Nineteen sixty-three to sixty-seven . . . Yes, yes; I remember you. On your first day here you created a ruckus and had to be punished. I remember it well. What have you done for yourself over the years? Have you learned to curb your temper?"

Amazing! They always remember the negatives. She didn't remember that I ". . . read very well for someone from Jamaica" and was always in the top three in my class.

"Well, Miss . . ." *Miss? Did I think I was back in school? Mind you, it bloody well feels like it . . .* "Well Miss, I'm pleased to inform you that I consider myself successful in that I have achieved my career goals, and have developed into a strong independent person. I know my rights and stand up for them, and *still* take truck and nonsense from no-one, as I *did not* on my first day here, as you remember. As for my temper, it is kept firmly in check, unless the situation calls for it to be otherwise!"

Oh dear; I hadn't meant to sound so caustic. I relax my voice and my stance and continue. "Thank you, Miss

Fishpoole, for your part in shaping me into the person I am today."

Well, so much for the old school and Miss Fishpoole/ Anderson. They served their purpose in my life, making their own little contributions, whether positive or negative. They gave me my first valuable experiences of life among a race of people who were not my own.

I augmented what they had taught me with what I had learned from my friend Mr Long Neck Man, and my general observation of life. I had worked hard, and achieved, and now I was about to realise my dream—homeward bound, Jamaica way.

I made my silent goodbyes to the ghosts of my childhood; the old man's beard, the harebells, woodbine and bluebells; the brook, the woods and crab-apple trees; the playground and the conker tree where the tyre swing used to hang; Mr Long Neck Man and his big old empty house, and the old hollow oak tree that was no more.

A real pity about that old oak tree. A real pity.

19 RETURNING RESIDENT

The sun rose over the hilltop in a glorious burst of fiery colour. The fresh sweet scent of the Jamaican morning permeated the air, while the gently blowing breeze fanned the foliage which was still wet with the early morning dew, and a chorus of bird and insect song made music for the ears.

The middle-aged woman, who was watching the sunrise, inhaled a deep breath of the pure sweet air and expelled it in a sigh of utter satisfaction and contentment. Here she was at last, home in Jamaica where she belonged, and where she had longed to be all through those hard cold years in England.

They had not been easy, those years. Trudging through the freezing cold snow, with the icy wind cutting like a knife and freezing her fingers and toes, despite socks, boots and gloves.

And then there had been the work. The residents in the old people's home where she had worked assumed that their age and colour gave them licence to physically and verbally abuse her, and of course she could not retaliate. Even when they spat at her and called her "nigger" or "black bastard" or told her to go back to her jungle, she could do nothing but

grit her teeth and carry on. There were even times when human excrement and urine were thrown at her. There was no point in complaining to the management; they always said the same thing. "You should know, Mrs Pennycook, these patients are old and senile and have lost their capacity for rational behaviour . . ."

Some of the patients, though quite mobile and able to walk or wheel themselves to the toilet, deliberately fouled themselves so that she would have to clean them up and bathe them. Nobody could tell her that some of them did not do it deliberately for the express purpose of making her have to clean them. Sometimes, being only human, she was seriously tempted to ill-treat some of them, but it was only that—a temptation—for she was a God-fearing Christian woman; but some other members of staff were not . . .

And to make things worse, the pay had hardly been sufficient to provide for her family *and* save to build a house in Jamaica, which was the original reason she had gone to England in the first place, so she was forced to work as much overtime as she could get, since her husband was not pulling his weight financially, and spent most of his earnings at the pub and the bookmaker's or sporting with his friends.

That had placed a lot of strain on her family life. She was permanently tired and frustrated, and as a result was often irritable with the children; shouting at them and slapping them for minor things. Eventually she had decided that she was better off without the husband, and the marriage had ended in divorce, leaving her on her own with five children to bring up.

But, to her way of thinking, the most unfair thing about the whole situation had been the fact that too much responsibility had been placed on the shoulders of her daughter, who had, in effect, taken on the role of mother to her four younger brothers. From the age of eleven or so, Cherry had practically run the home; cooking, washing, cleaning, ironing; with only minimal help from the boys.

The woman shook her head as if to ward off the unpleasant thoughts. No point looking back. Her children were all grown up now; all had good jobs and were leading happy and contented lives. And God help her, she would never again have to clean up white people shit and suffer their abuse. She had got what she wanted from England; a nice home in Jamaica, and a regular income in the shape of her pension, which would be paid in English pounds every month for the rest of her life.

And she deserved every penny of it; it had been hard earned. But now those long hard years of struggle were finally over, and she, Imogene Pennycook, at long last could relax and enjoy her island which she had left some forty years ago as a young woman.

But there was still a small cloud on the horizon. She still had one more battle to fight. She was having considerable difficulty with one of the tenants who had been renting her home. But Almighty God would eventually take care of that situation; she wasn't going to let it mar her joy at being home.

She surveyed her domain with pleasure. She had a beautiful house, situated on two acres of gently rolling land, with a river sealing the southern boundary, and the main road from Spanish Town to Old Harbour fronting the northern edge. To the east and west, her neighbours' houses were within hailing distance, but not so close as to be intrusive.

She had been extremely lucky to get the two acres in its entirety; the owner had been about to sub-divide into four half-acre lots and she had had to pay him far more than she felt the land to be worth in order to keep it intact. But she had not regretted it for an instant. She had had her house built, and the surrounding land planted with marketable produce such as coconuts, plantains and bananas, ackee, breadfruit, mangos, limes and other citrus. She also had a section of 'cash crops' such as peppers, callaloo, pak choy, okra, and so on. She had reserved a good quarter acre to lay out her beautiful flower garden which was her pride and joy.

The house itself, a five bedroomed single storey dwelling, was built on a small rise, overlooking the main road. A hundred yard driveway, lined by Christmas Palms, led from the large double gates to the house. A good sized front lawn—with borders of croton, bougainvillea, and hibiscus—boasted two mango trees with a hammock strung between them.

It was a large house, commonly known as a 'two family residence.' It was built so as to be able to house two families without each getting in the other's way. This was a popular way of generating extra income, as one side of the house could be rented out. It consisted of a large living/dining room which separated the two sides of the house. Each side had its own kitchen and laundry rooms. One side had two rooms and a bathroom, while the other side had the master bedroom with on-suite bath, and two other bedrooms which shared a bathroom. A long front veranda, incorporating a car port, ran the length of the house, and of course, being Jamaica, the whole was enclosed by a steel security grille.

Both sides of the house were tenanted and both tenants had been given notice to vacate the premises. Penny only needed one side vacant but she had given both tenants notice. When one moved, she would withdraw the other's notice. If the tenant on the smaller side moved first, she would relocate the other tenant from the big side of the house. However, both sets of tenants were still in residence; rented accommodation was extremely hard to find, and expensive too. That wasn't the problem. Penny could understand and sympathise with their situation, and had been willing to allow them the time needed to sort themselves out. It was a large house, and would accommodate them all comfortably, with a bit of give and take, until one of them could secure alternative accommodation.

But when a tenant has the gall to curse you in your own house, and tell you that you can't get them out—well, that is a different something!

They had known she was coming; they had been given six months notice, but Penny had been well aware that there was no guarantee they would have gone by the time she got there. However, she had been quite willing to live in one room and share kitchen facilities with the tenant, to give them the time needed.

She had arrived at the house in a very good mood, feeling exultant to be home. When she got there only one of the tenants was at home. Mrs Miller, who lived on the smaller side of the house, was a dressmaker, and worked from home. She explained to Penny that she had not yet found anywhere to move to, but was looking in earnest. Penny told her that if she could "make herself small" to create some space for Penny to put some of her things when they arrived, they could co-exist until Mrs Miller found somewhere.

Penny's sense of well-being was shattered when the other tenant came home. Barbara Lewin was a totally different character to Mrs Jean Miller. Penny had not met either of them before, as the house had been looked after and rented out by her father.

Miss Lewin did not greet and approach her in the same civil manner as Mrs Miller had done. When Mrs Miller introduced Penny to Miss Lewin, her response was far from civil. "A-hoa; yu come? Mi nuh fine nuh-weh yet, suh yu gwine haffi wait fi di place."

Penny was rather taken aback by this approach. Miss Lewin's stance and tone were aggressive, and her voice conveyed dislike; for what reason, Penny knew not, since she had never met the woman before. She replied civilly to the woman.

"Well, Miss Lewin, my furniture will be arriving in about two week's time, so if yu could "small up yuself" like Miss Miller so I can get some space . . ."

She was rudely interrupted. "What yu mean yu furniture a-arrive? Yu tink yu kyaan juss move een pon people suh? Mi have rights, y'nuh. Mi know mi rights!"

Penny was beginning to get annoyed, but she held on to her temper and tried again. "I just need one room; the master bedroom big enough fi hold my tings, and what can't hold can go on the car-port, suh if yu could juss move out yu things from into the master bedroom . . ."

Again she was interrupted by Miss Lewin. "Move dem out? Move dem out guh weh? Is waan yu waan put mi a-road? Well, wi wi' si what di Rent Board have to seh bout dat!"

Penny finally lost her temper. "Yu have rights? Mi have rights to'. This is *my* house, and yu get proper notice; more dan the law stipulate. Now, my furniture is coming in two weeks, and A want somewhere to put them and somewhere to sleep. The living room more dan big enough fi yu bed and whatever else yu have in *my* bedroom. And oh; A gwine to be sharing yu kitchen to!"

With that she had turned her back on Barbara Lewin, bid good-day to Mrs Miller, and strode down the driveway and through the gate to wait for a taxi on the road. She had been seething with anger. How dare that woman tell her she could not move into her own-a house! Well we would soon see whose house it was!

She had taken a commuter taxi into Spanish Town and purchased a sofa-bed. She found a truck for hire, and rode in it back to Old Harbour where she went to her father's house where she had been staying since arriving on the island two days previously. She packed up her belongings and put them in the truck, as she explained to her father what had transpired at her house.

It had not been her intention to move into her house until her furniture arrived, but Miss Lewin's attitude had 'gotten her back up.' She would move into her house this very day, and let anyone try to stop her!

She had enlisted the help of some of her nephews, and they had moved Miss Lewin's things from the master bedroom and placed them in the living room. Then they had moved in her sofa-bed and the few things she had brought from her father's house, and one of her nephews had changed the locks on the bedroom doors. She would start sleeping in her house, but would continue to eat at her father's until her stove arrived.

Miss Lewin had not been at home when Penny and her nephews had arrived. They had put the things into the house and left. Penny had returned to Old Harbour to eat her dinner, and then returned to the house to spend the night.

Early in the pre-dawn the next day, Penny had gone outside to watch the sun rise and enjoy the freshness of the Jamaican morning. This was one of the things she had dreamed about while in England; to wake up early because she wanted to, and not because she had to, and to watch the sun come up. She would waste none of this precious time thinking about Barbara Lewin; she would deal with her later.

As she turned to go back into the house, she heard a shout from the gate. "Auntie P, yu deh yah?" It was one of her nephews who was known as "Dread" because he was a dreadlocked Rastaman. "Si mi here," she called, walking from around the side of the house to meet him on the driveway. "Morning, Dread; how yu do?"

"I man hearty, Auntie; what a gwaan?"

He told her he had heard about what had transpired the previous day, and how she had decided to move into her house straight away. "Dah gyal deh nuh easy," he told Penny. "I man know har; yu haffi careful wid har; might be it hood-a better ef yu wait tell shi move out."

Penny was not intimidated. "I'm not afraid of her. I have a right to be in mi own-a house."

"Well, ahright den," Dread said. "A wi' mek di ress a fambly know seh yu deh yah, suh dat dem kyan keep a eye pon yu and di gyal. Shi betta watch harself; A doan't waan haffi damage har."

Penny felt good knowing that she had 'backative' in case of trouble with Barbara Lewin. After Dread had left, she knocked on Mrs Miller's door, which was opened by her sixteen year old daughter, Teneisha. "Maaning, Mrs Pennycook; Moomy in di kitchen," the girl said politely.

Penny walked through the house to Mrs Miller's kitchen. She knocked at the kitchen door and called, "Mrs Miller? Good morning. Could I have a word with yu, please?" Mrs Miller came to the open kitchen door. "Maaning, Miss Pennycook; please to come inside. Can I offer yu a likkle breakfast?"

"Oh, yes; thank yu, that would be very nice."

She sat on the chair indicated by Mrs Miller and was handed a plate of fried dumplings with callaloo and plantain, and a cup of mint tea. While she ate, they discussed the temporary living arrangements. Jean Miller was very helpful and readily agreed to share her kitchen facilities with Penny, although it was on the opposite side of the house, but Penny did not relish using the same kitchen as Barbara Lewin.

Penny thanked Jean for her courtesy and kindness, and told her that she could stop searching for alternative accommodation as she, Penny, was withdrawing her notice. Mrs Miller could stay; there was no way Penny would ever contemplate living in the same house as Barbara Lewin.

They talked for a while and then Penny went outside to relax in the hammock which Dread had hung for her. She had not seen Barbara that morning. Apparently she had either not spent the night at home, or she had left before daybreak. Her three children had gotten themselves ready for school, and left, giving Penny a brief "good morning" as they passed her on their way to the gate.

The next few days passed uneventfully. Penny got on very well with Mrs Miller and Teneisha, and was pleasant to Miss Lewin's children, who were pleasant to her when their mother was not around, but reticent and unresponsive when she was. Barbara herself was surly and pointedly ignored Penny, acting as if she did not exist, which was fine by Penny; she had nothing to say to her either. She just wanted her out.

One afternoon Penny was swinging in her hammock under the cool shade of the mango trees, when she heard a knocking on the gate. She got up and went to see who it was.

"Aftanoon, Mam. A looking fah Miss Imogene Pennycook." It was a uniformed police officer. "That's me; how can I help you?" Penny was curious. Why on earth would a police officer be asking to see her?

He handed her a document and asked her to sign the receipt. She looked at the paper and realised that it was a court summons. "What is this?" she asked in surprise, looking askance at the officer.

"Am juss a messenger, Mam; read it and si," and with that he turned and walked away.

Penny shook her head. He didn't have to be quite so brusque, but no problem. She returned to her seat under the mango tree and examined the document in detail, exclaiming in disbelief. It was a summons to appear in front of the Rent Assessment Board; she had been accused of charging an excessive rent for the rooms and of threatening to put Barbara Lewin and her belongings out on the street.

Penny's blood was boiling. How dare that maaga foot gyal guh tell such barefaced lies on her? She got up and went marching into the house. "Miss Barbara! Miss Barbara! A word with you, please," she called. Barbara came and stood in the doorway of the living room.

"What yu waant?" she demanded. Penny thrust the summons at her. "What is the meaning of this? When did I threaten to throw you out?" She was so angry she was trembling.

Barbara glanced at the summons and handed it back. "Well," she said in an unnecessarily loud and aggressive tone, "if yu moving in yu tings, is put yu putting mi out. Mi is a legal tenant inside here, and mi have mi rights. Yu kyaan' just come move een pon people suh . . ."

She went on to curse Penny at the top of her voice, punctuating the sentences with disgusting swear words. She accused Penny of thinking she "was nice" because she had been in England and could afford to buy a big house down here. Penny was not going to take this lying down. No sir!

She drew herself up to her full height and commenced to verbally chastise Barbara Lewin. "Gyal, guh wash out yu dutty mout' wid carbolic soap! Yu nuh have nuh mannahs nor nuh breeding! Mi come here wid good intention; all mi ask is dat yu small up yuself suh dat mi kyan get one likkle katch till yu fine someweh. Is a big house, and all a wi kyan hole quite comfatable wid a bit a give and tek.

"Mi nevah have nuh intention fi put yu a street, and yu well know it. Now yu waan come tell mi seh mi nuh have nuh right ovah mi own-a house weh mi struggle and sweat fi buy; an a come trett'n fi put mi a prison.

"When time mi did a struggle chew sleet and snow fi guh clean up white people shit, which part yu did deh, eeh? An nung yu come a tell mi bout yu have right. Yu waan come tun queen eena adda people castle!

"Well, a fi-mi castle dis an a mi a di queen een ya, an mi naa mek yu come rule mi eena mi own-a roose, suh di bess ting yu kyan do is look to reap di fruit a yu own-a layba and leff mi fi enjoy my own weh mi wuk suh lang an hard fah!"

While Penny had been speaking Barbara had carried on cursing but Penny hadn't paused long enough for anything Barbara said to penetrate. It is doubtful whether Barbara heard much of Penny's tirade either, however, Penny felt much better for having gotten it off her chest.

The noise of the argument had drawn Jean to the doorway of her apartment which opened onto the veranda. Now, as Penny turned her back on Miss Barbara and strode away, Jean asked her quietly what had happened. Penny explained about the summons from the Rent Board.

Jean did not show any surprise. "Dat gyal wi do anyting, and tell any amount a lie fi get weh she want. She-a one big mout bully, but one teacha did tell mi seh di emptiest vessel mek di most nize. All shi kyan do is shout an cuss up whole-heap a badwud, but in di enn, she know seh she haffi come out-a yu place.

"Is shame she shame mek she deh gwaan suh, far shi give everybaddy di impression dat is she own dis house; but now story come to bump. She nevah remembah seh one day, one day, yu would-a come-come mash up har dally house, and now everybaddy a guh know seh a pose she did a pose, and she's ongle a tenant after all.

"She have some big frien' weh she deh cultivate; Councillor Dis and Councillor Dat an Memba a parlament Suh and Suh. Mek dem show dem friendship now, an help har fine a katch."

Jean went on to tell Penny that Barbara Lewin had been on the verge of being put on the street by court bailiffs after her previous land-lord had been trying to evict her for a year. "Yu faada rent har di place too quick; him should-a aaks roun' bout har furse."

Penny replied, "Well I don't intend to wait a year. I am going to see a lawyer first thing in the morning."

True to her word, the next morning she went into Old Harbour to consult with a lawyer. When she explained her situation, he was not able to offer her much reassurance. He told her that the whole process of eviction could take some considerable time, because the magistrate was obliged to give the tenant sufficient time to find alternative accommodation.

Penny was aghast. "And in the meantime *I* must find alternative accommodation, or else put up with facetiness and inconvenience in my own home? What kind of justice is that? No wonder people don't want to rent out dem place, if dat is how di law deal with them. Imagine dat! People nuh have nuh right ovah dem own-a property! From I was born . . . !"

Penny left the lawyers office feeling very depressed. How she had looked forward to coming home after all those horrible years in England. When she got home she knelt down and prayed long and hard, asking God to send a speedy resolution to her problem.

She felt much refreshed after her communion with God, and went into the kitchen to prepare something for her dinner. She found Jean in there, and told her what the lawyer had said. "But I'm not going to spoil my homecoming by worrying about it," she told Jean. "I'm just going to act as if she doesn't exist, and get on with doing what I came home to do—relax and take things easy. I'm going to walk out my two acres, paint my house, go to the beach; all the things I have been looking forward to for the past thirty odd years."

After dinner that evening Penny walked a short distance on her land till she came to a spot where she could watch the setting sun slide behind the distant hills to the west of where she was standing. She sat on a rock and enjoyed the cool evening breeze as she savoured the pleasant feeling of well-being that had been with her since talking to God this afternoon. She wasn't going to be depressed; no sir—she had worked hard; she intended to enjoy it for as long as God put breath in her body.

Barbara Lewin and people like her could go to hell as far as she was concerned—and probably would, too!

"I can well understand," Penny thought to herself, "why so many returning residents who have come home 'for good' go running back to 'Foreign.'" She reflected on what she had experienced since coming home. Shop assistants were slow to serve and generally impolite; they would stand talking to their friends while you waited to be served, and if you dared to interrupt they would tell you that if you can't wait, go elsewhere!

Police officers were no better. They felt themselves to be above the rest of the community—rather like how the house slaves had felt themselves above the field slaves during that infamous period of our history. Of course, there were exceptions to this general rule; Penny realised that she could not tar every individual with the same brush, but unfortunately, the 'good' ones seemed to be in the minority.

One thing was certain. Penny intended to write to all her friends in England and tell them—if you intend to come home anytime soon, give your tenants notice NOW! Otherwise you may find them still in residence when you arrive, and have the devil of a time shifting them.

Penny reflected unhappily on how unfair it was that the good had to suffer for the bad. She was sure there were a lot of good decent tenants, but people like Barbara Lewin made things difficult for everyone. The law, too, seemed to slant in favour of the tenants over the owners, which was so unfair. After all, many of these owners had spent years in cold climates and unpleasant working conditions in order to have been able to purchase their properties, and they had every right to be able to enjoy the fruits of their labour.

As the evening began to turn into night and Penny began to retrace her steps back to the house, she fervently gave God thanks for bringing her home, and vowed that she would not be one of the many returning residents who went scurrying back to the frigid lands which had taken the best years of their lives while they strived to build something of value to return to in their native lands. England had taken the best thirty-odd years of her life, and now all she wanted to do was to relax and enjoy what she had worked so hard for.

Yes, she was finally home for good, and no amount of Barbara Lewins, or impolite shop assistants or public servants were going to send her running back to the cold. No sir! This returning resident was returned for good!

ABOUT THE AUTHOR

Claudette Beckford-Brady is an award-winning novelist and short-story writer. She was born in Old Harbour, Jamaica, where she spent the first seven years of her life before going to join her parents who had migrated to the United Kingdom leaving her in the care of her great-grandmother. She learned to read at her great-gran's knee and it was there she developed the love of reading which has stayed with her throughout her life. At some point during her early years it occurred to her that she could perhaps write as good as, if not better, than some of the authors she was reading and this inspired her to start writing short stories. She began entering her stories in literary competitions in 1991 where she achieved great success, winning a number of awards. Two of her award winning short stories are featured in The Gold Anthology, which is a collection of award winning entries from the Jamaica Cultural Development Commission's annual literary competition. Claudette also has three published novels.

OTHER BOOKS BY CLAUDETTE BECKFORD-BRADY

<u>SWEET HOME, JAMAICA:</u>

Michelle Freeman, affectionately known as Shell or Shellie, was born in Jamaica but migrated to England with her parents at the age of three. At age thirteen her life is thrown into turmoil when she accidentally discovers that her father's wife, whom she had always taken for granted as being her mother, is in fact, not. This shocking discovery leads her to begin a search for her biological mother. The search eventually takes her to Jamaica where she finds a large extended maternal family and develops a deep and abiding love for the island of her birth. After leaving school and university in London, where she studied journalism, Shellie decides to leave the UK and practise her profession in Jamaica. However, all is not plain sailing, as she encounters culture shock, prejudice and jealousy and comes to the realisation that her beloved island is not the idyllic paradise she had supposed it to be. Set in South London and on the beautiful island of Jamaica, the story spans seventeen years, following the fiery and feisty young woman through her teenage years, young love and tragedy, and into adulthood and more conflicts and clashes.

"... one of the most powerful & poignant first novels to come from the Jamaican Diaspora in many years . . . . . showcases Beckford-Brady's creative talent as a writer and her deep perception of Jamaican society at home & abroad. A compellingly delicious "must read". **Hardbeat News & Caribbean Link, USA** *"An*

*instant classic. (Beckford-Brady's) . . . insight into character & motivation is flawless and her depiction of characters of all ages absolutely believable. She writes the story as if she were born to tell it. It makes for a wonderful read which leaves the reader breathless with its simplicity and positivity." **Sunday Observer Bookends Magazine (Jamaica)** "(Beckford-Brady) . . . "hijacks the reader's attention from the very first line and holds it throughout with a riveting portrayal of a young woman's journey into adulthood. **Jamrock Magazine: New York, USA***

THE MISSING YEARS

The Missing Years is the sequel to Beckford-Brady's first novel, **Sweet Home, Jamaica.** It concludes the saga of Michelle Freeman and her extended family.

The initial reunion with her biological mother was not the tear-jerker Michelle had expected so when the families came together for the five-yearly family reunion emotions were running high. Life for Michelle was already full, juggling a career as the co-owner of SmallRock Publications, plus family life, but things were about to be turned on their head. A bungled robbery, a dead youth and a usually devoted husband who has started staying out all night with no explanation . . . Is Michelle's husband getting too close to Delisia?

A poignant, heart-warming tale of family relationships and conflict resolution, spiced with fast-paced drama

RETURN TO FIDELITY

Edith Maynard-Livingstone is disenchanted with her fifteen-year marriage to Basil, who has a predilection toward girls young enough to be his daughters. However, Edith is not about to leave him and give up the comfortable lifestyle she has become accustomed to after having grown up dirt-poor in a rural Jamaican parish. However, when she runs into an old friend the temptation to give Basil a taste of his own medicine and have a fling is overwhelming.

Leroy Duncan has a happy marriage but lately a difference of opinion is threatening the relationship. Having lived in England for years, Leroy now wishes to return to Jamaica, but Evadne his wife has no such desire. She considers the island to be a backwater, lacking in modern amenities, full of criminal elements, and prone to natural disasters such as hurricanes and earthquakes. She fails to see why she should give up her comfortable existence in the UK for a life of uncertainty.

Set in the UK and the Jamaican parishes of St. Catherine and Trelawny this story gives an insightful and sometimes humorous look at the marital conflicts which can arise when couples find they no longer have the same objectives.

These books are all available on amazon in both paperback and Kindle formats. Sweet Home, Jamaica is available in paperback as a single volume or as a two-volume alternative. Visit the author's page at **www.amazon.com or www. amazon.co.uk**